XCalibur,
Merlin and the
Teeth of the Dragon

X Calibur, Merlin and the Teeth of the Dragon

David Morgan Williams

y Lolfa

THE SPIRIT OF THE DRAGON
A Celtic Odyssey

Book I – *Dragonrise*
Book II – *Ebony and Ivory*
Book III – *XCalibur, Merlin and the Teeth of the Dragon*

First impression: 2014

Cover illustration: Dylan Williams

ISBN: 978 184771 823 5

Published and printed in Wales
on paper from well-maintained forests by
Y Lolfa Cyf., Talybont, Ceredigion SY24 5HE
website www.ylolfa.com
e-mail ylolfa@ylolfa.com
tel 01970 832 304
fax 832 782

I dedicate this book to my family,
all of whom are very special to me

Acknowledgements

Thanks to my dear wife Jan for her continued encouragement, and for cajoling me into finishing the trilogy.

I owe a great debt of gratitude to my son Chris, and daughter Ceri for typing the manuscript and to my new young friend Jason for finishing it off. Chris also agreed to coordinate everything before dispatching it to my publisher. Diolch yn fawr iawn!

Although the three stories in the 'Spirit of the Dragon' trilogy are works of fiction, I have endeavoured to make all historical references and geographical locations as accurate as possible. Any errors in these are entirely mine. I would like to express my sincere thanks to the following sources which have been invaluable during my research: *King Arthur: Dark Age Warrior and Mythic Hero* by John Matthews; *The Terracotta Army* by John Man; *An Introduction to Celtic Mythology* by David Bellingham; and *The Literature of Wales* by Dafydd Johnston. My thanks to all of the above for any copyright material, such as quotations, which might appear in the text.

My sincere thanks to Garmon Gruffudd (MD); my editors: Lefi Gruffudd (Chief) and especially Eirian Jones (English language editor) for her helpful and constructive comments during the final stages of preparation and proof reading. Also all the 'behind the scenes staff' at Y Lolfa, particularly Alan Thomas for his endless patience and creativity in designing the book itself – diolch yn fawr iawn!

A big thank you to Josh for his awesome vision of the dragon spirit. Finally, a special thank you to Dylan Williams for his inspiring and exciting cover design work.

The story so far...

In Book I, ***Dragonrise***, Huw is in a state of inner turmoil. His mother
Beth, a policewoman, has recently been killed while attempting to
apprehend a group of men who had broken in to a local armaments'
factory. He is highly vulnerable and sensitive to what is happening
around him, especially the disturbances taking place at the ancient
burial mound, Twmp Trelech.

He is soon brought face to face with the forces of good and evil
and, with his cousin Arthur and friend Samantha (Sam), he relives
part of the legend of Culwch and Olwen, one of the great stories
of Celtic mythology and one of the earliest in which King Arthur
appears.

Huw, Arthur and Sam, with a lot of help from the dragon spirit,
eventually overcome enormous odds to defeat a cell of terrorists
which has been operating undercover in their locality. However,
they have no way of knowing that the real conflict was only just
beginning.

In Book II, ***Ebony and Ivory***, the scene switches to Dubai,
in the United Arab Emirates. Sam's mother, Mary Grant, who is a
horse owner, is invited by Sheikh Rashid to visit and enter her prize-
winning horse, Ivory, in the Dubai World Cup, the richest horse race
in the world.

Soon after they arrive in Dubai, Huw and Ivory, together with
Sheikh Rashid's horse Ebony, are kidnapped. Huw eventually
discovers that he has been imprisoned in the dungeon of an ancient
fortress. He is in deep despair until he realises that his imprisonment

was witnessed by Ahmed, a young Bedouin shepherd boy. Ahmed and his sister, Sheba, seek advice from their tribal chief, El Sufi, who was also a magician. Together they work out a plan to help Huw escape with the horses and hide in a secret cave.

Soon they are pursued by Badrag, their captor, who calls on the evil desert djinn (genie), Jackaala, who is able to change his shape at will. It changes into a three-headed serpent to try and prevent Huw and his friends from escaping. But El Sufi has given Huw an ancient spear with magical properties, and with the help of Draco, the dragon spirit, together they destroy the evil Djinn.

They were safe again for now, but the conflict is far from over. Now read on...

Map of China

Key : ▲ – Highest Mts.
△△ – Other high mountains.
▦ – Desert Areas.
● – Main locations in story.

'Never laugh at live dragons.'

J. R. R. Tolkien – *The Hobbit* (1937)

'You see, but you do not observe.'

Arthur Conan Doyle – 'A Scandal in Bohemia',
The Adventures of Sherlock Holmes (1891)

'All for one, one for all.'

Alexandre Dumas, *père* – *The Three Musketeers* (1844)

The Spirit of the DRAGON

Designed by Joshua Williams,
the author's eldest grandson

Chapter 1

Aneurin

Although Mary had decided two years ago to give the new young foal, XCalibur, to Sheikh Rashid as a special gift, the sheikh had asked if the foal could remain with his mother, Ivory, until he became a colt. The sheikh also knew how much it meant to Huw, Arthur, and Sam to watch him growing up and helping to care for him.

It was early on a Saturday morning and, after a quick breakfast, Huw had gone straight to the stables at Grant Court where his father Mike Pendry was the head trainer. He had already asked his Dad if he could prepare XCalibur for his morning exercise, and now he was busy getting him ready. As he moved around the colt checking his legs were in perfect condition, something glinted in the corner of his eye. The sunlight shining through the stable window had landed on the medallion which Huw had first discovered at the burial mound, Twmp Trelech. Now it was attached to the original bridle hanging up nearby, which had adorned Culhwch's horse when he had first visited King Arthur's court in the sixth century. As there was still half an hour to go before the exercise gallop was due to start, Huw decided to try the bridle on XCalibur to see how well it would fit on the shiny black colt. It was almost a perfect fit, with the bridle decorated in embossed gold, together with the girdle which supported the medallion on the horse's chest.

Huw stroked the white sword-shaped blaze on the colt's head with his right hand whilst simultaneously holding the bridle in his left. His body trembled, and a powerful force surged through him. There was a sudden whoosh of air, and he found himself whirling head first through a long dark tunnel. Although he didn't lose consciousness, he found it difficult to think straight, but he could feel XCalibur alongside him, and it was instinct that made him cling tightly to the horse's bridle, and swing his leg over the horse's back into the saddle, where he clung on for dear life. Several minutes seemed to pass, and then a strange blue light appeared at the end of the dark tunnel. The light grew nearer and stronger, and suddenly they burst out of the tunnel and collapsed in a heap on the edge of a large field surrounded by thick woodland. The noise was deafening. Men were shouting and screaming. Horses were neighing and whinnying. Sword clashed upon sword, shield against shield, and lance against lance. Wherever they were – they were on the edge of a battlefield.

A very young man in battle dress, but not wearing heavy armour spotted Huw, and pulled him towards a thick clump of trees.

"Quick, behind here," he said, "before you are seen by the enemy."

"Who are the enemy?" asked Huw.

"Why, the Dirians and Bernicians of course! Sworn enemies of the Gododdin."

"The Gododdin! But who are they?"

"My tribe, of course, from up North."

"So where are we now?"

"Don't know much do you," said the sturdy, dark-haired youth.

"Come to think of it, you don't seem to belong here at all. Are you foreign?"

"No," replied Huw still in a state of confusion.

"I was just about to take my colt out for his morning exercises, when something strange happened, and now I'm here. Where is this place?" Huw's voice rose anxiously.

"Hey, keep your voice down, or they'll be onto us. If you really don't know, then I'd better tell you. This is Catraeth [Catterick] in North Yorkshire, and if you hadn't already realised it, there's a battle going on."

"A battle?" said Huw, "but I don't understand."

"You must be concussed. Here, let me help you. That's my job anyway, looking after the wounded. 'Cause I'm only 17, they won't let me fight."

"What's your name?" asked Huw.

"Aneurin," said the young man, "and who are you?"

"Huw… Huw Pendry… I live in the lodge of Grant Court. My Dad is Head Trainer at the stables there."

"Trainer for what?"

"He trains horses for racing."

"You must be very concussed, jabbering on about horse training," said Aneurin anxiously. "Here, drink some water from this flask, sit down, and put this blanket around you until you regain your senses."

Aneurin's eyes alighted on the colt, and he gazed in wonder at the beautiful condition of his black coat, and the unusual white blaze on his head. Then he noticed the horse's golden bridle, and began to realise this was no ordinary horse, and it hadn't just come off the battlefield either. It was not lathered in sweat, it wasn't breathing heavily, and there were no visible cuts or bruises.

"You weren't on the battlefield were you!" said Aneurin.

"No, I told you I was about to take XCalibur for his morning exercises, when something strange happened. We were pitched into a long dark tunnel, and we had no sense of time. When we eventually left the tunnel…"

"Hold on a minute, did you say Excalibur?"

"Yes."

"So did you name him after King Arthur's sword then?"

"Well, yes, as you can see his blaze is shaped just like a sword, but there's a bit more to it than that."

Huw explained to Aneurin how he had first discovered the medallion at the ancient burial mound near his home, and how they had later identified it as part of the bridle belonging to Culhwch, King Arthur's cousin.

"Did you say that you found it at an ancient burial mound?"

"Yes, that's right."

"That's strange, because only yesterday I spoke to Merlin who told me that the burial mound was secure and heavily guarded to prevent grave robbers from breaking in."

"Did you say Merlin? He's around here then?"

"Yes, he's not far away when there's a battle. He's usually on hand to give advice."

"I think I'm beginning to understand what's happened. You said earlier that I didn't seem to belong here. Well I know this is going to sound stupid, but I think I've come here from a different time."

"And what time would that be?" asked Aneurin looking alarmed.

"2012," said Huw.

"What, that's impossible, this is only 590 AD."

"I told you it would sound stupid, didn't I."

"Look, I think I have an idea," said Aneurin. "You stay here undercover, and I'll go and find Merlin and bring him here. He'll be able to advise us what to do. Now remember, stay where you are, and be as quiet as possible. I will be back soon."

"Promise me you'll be back. I'm really scared now."

"I promise, don't worry, I won't desert you. Here, you can read some of my verses while I'm gone. It's a hobby of mine, keeping a record of what happens at the scene of battle."

Aneurin then disappeared through the shrubbery, leaving Huw holding a sheaf of grubby papers.

Chapter 2

The Empty Stable

On Saturday, 9 December, Arthur finished his breakfast and said goodbye to his parents, Rachel and Morgan. He set off from Pendry Farm, perched high on the ridge of Mynydd Mawr, and began the long walk down to the stables at Grant Court, where he had arranged to meet Huw for morning exercises. He had to walk carefully this particular morning, because there was still a great deal of snow lying on the mountain road, compacted and icy. The gritting lorries never reached this far up, and only four wheel drives could attempt the journey, as the road was steep in parts.

Although it could be treacherous for many, Arthur loved to see the snow on the mountainside. Everything looked so white and pure, and there was a wonderful stillness in the air. A light breeze occasionally sent whispers of snow fanning out from the branches of trees and hedges that lined the road. Everything looked so different in the snow, as winter re-clothed the landscape as only she can.

When he arrived at the stables, he found XCalibur's stable door open, but there was no sign of Huw or the colt. Arthur frowned at the sight of the empty stable, as this was not what he had expected to find. He searched around looking for a note, or some sign from Huw, as to where he might be. Something glinted on a table at the far side of the stable. It was Huw's mobile phone. Arthur was even more mystified as he knew Huw would not normally leave the stables without it. He switched the phone on, but there was no message. Arthur looked around the stable and sensed there was an eerie silence in the place. He began to shiver, although he wasn't cold after his long walk down from the farm. Then he noticed something *really* odd. One of the stable walls was glowing with a cold blue light, and it seemed to be slowly pulsating. Arthur closed his eyes and shook his head as if to clear his vision, but when he reopened them, the blue light was still there. He walked gingerly across to the wall and reached out to touch it. His fingers tingled, and he felt some kind of force running up his arm. He pulled his hand away quickly, as if he had just touched something really hot, and then stepped back to ponder on what lay before him.

Arthur decided to call Huw's father Mike at the lodge, on his mobile.

"Hello, Mike Pendry speaking."

"Hi there, Uncle Mike, it's Arthur. Do you know where Huw might be? He's not at the stables, and there's no sign of XCalibur either!"

"That's odd. I don't think he would have left for exercises without you."

"No, that's what I can't understand, and there's no note or anything, only his mobile."

"His mobile! He wouldn't ride off on his own without that. Something's wrong. Wait there Arthur, I'll be straight over!"

Mike arrived on the scene about five minutes later, and began to look around the empty stable with Arthur.

"That's really odd," said Mike.

"What is it?"

"The golden bridle's missing too."

"But I thought either you or Henry would have returned it to Grant Court after the photo shoot yesterday," said Arthur.

"We were in a hurry and decided to leave it here overnight, thinking it would be perfectly safe. But maybe we were wrong to do that."

"Why were you having a photo shoot?" asked Arthur

"So we could send some up-to-date photographs of XCalibur to Sheikh Rashid. We thought it might be a good idea to show him wearing the golden bridle."

"Don't suppose Huw could have borrowed it could he?"

"You mean put it on XCalibur, and then go off on his exercises alone. No, that's not like Huw, but…?" Mike hesitated.

"What is it?"

"That wall over there… it's glowing!"

"Yes, I was just about to mention that Uncle Mike. It's glowing with a cold blue light, and there's something else."

"What?"

"It tingles when you touch it."

"*Tingles*?"

"Yes, go ahead and see for yourself, it doesn't really hurt much."

Mike stepped cautiously towards the wall, and reached out to touch it.

"Blimey, it's alive!" he said, feeling a force shooting up his arm. "What on earth's going on. This is ridiculous!"

"Arthur, would you mind waiting here to see if Huw returns? I shall go as fast as I can to Grant Court to see Mary and Henry and tell them what's happened. I'd prefer to talk to them face to face, rather than use the mobile. I'll be back as quickly as I can Arthur, and I'll bring some hot drinks with me. Will that be OK?"

"You bet," said Arthur, with one of his broad grins, "and don't forget the chocolate biscuits."

Mike smiled half-heartedly, and hurried off to the big house with a sinking feeling in the pit of his stomach.

Chapter 3

A surprise invitation

Mary Grant, the owner of the Grant (formerly Kervlan) Court Estate and Horse Racing Stables, heard the sound of a letter dropping through the letterbox as she came downstairs into the hall. Her pulse quickened when she saw the colour of the envelope, the colours of the Godolphin Stable. It was a letter from Sheikh Rashid. She hurried into the dining room where Henry and Sam (Samantha) were already having breakfast. She sat at the table and opened the envelope.

"What is it Mum?" asked Sam eagerly.

Mary quickly scanned the letter and with mounting excitement in her voice, replied, "It's an invitation from Sheikh Rashid asking us if we would like to take Ivory and XCalibur to Hong Kong for two big international races at the Sha Tin Racecourse."

"Wow," exclaimed Sam, "will it be soon?"

"Yes, very soon. He's sending a private jet tomorrow, to take us to Dubai and then on to Hong Kong."

Before they had time to take in the news, they heard a knock on the front door, and the sounds of voices as the housekeeper, Mrs Field, ushered Mike into the hall. She took him immediately to the dining room.

"Good morning Mike," said Henry, "would you like to join us for breakfast?"

"No thanks, Henry," he said, "I'm feeling rather anxious at the moment, as Huw and XCalibur are missing from the stables."

"What?" said Henry, "but surely they can't have gone very far."

"Where's Arthur?" asked Mary.

"He's keeping watch at the stables right now, but the strange thing is that he's been there since early morning and there's been no sign of Huw or XCalibur whatsoever."

"That's odd," said Sam, "because Huw would normally never leave on exercises without Arthur."

"That's right," said Mike, "and we've searched around the perimeter of the estate, but there are no signs of them anywhere."

"Oh, this is really bad news," said Mary holding up the letter, "especially as we've just received an invitation from Sheikh Rashid to join him in Hong Kong for the Hong Kong Challenge Gold Cup and Junior Cup. I'll have to call him straight away and explain that we won't be able to join him after all."

"No, there's no need to do that," said Mike. "I'm sure he'll turn up eventually, and there's a perfectly logical reason for what's happened. But, right now, it's a complete mystery."

"Is anything else missing from the stable?" asked Henry, thinking to himself about the golden bridle.

"I expect you're wondering about the bridle," replied Mike, picking up the vibes from Henry. "That's missing too, which is really odd, because Huw would never knowingly have removed it."

"No, no! They couldn't have been kidnapped again could they?" cried Sam.

Mike's face crumpled, as the full impact of Sam's words struck home. "I never gave that a thought." He looked forlorn.

"If that was the case," said Henry, "then surely there'd be tyre marks or other signs outside the stable. I don't think that's likely somehow – you'd have noticed."

Mike nodded and felt a little easier. "I'll phone Arthur now, and ask him to take another look outside, and also tell him about the invitation from Sheikh Rashid." He took out his mobile phone, called Arthur and gave him the message.

"I think you should proceed to Hong Kong, and as soon as we've sorted this out we'll follow."

Mary and Henry listened reluctantly to this plan, but Sam had a strong premonition that something very strange had happened.

"Apart from the missing bridle," asked Sam, "was there anything else which seemed unusual about the stable? It just doesn't add up!"

"Well, er, there was something else. I'd completely forgotten about it until you jogged my memory."

"What was it?"

"One of the walls of the stable was glowing with a strange blue light."

"A blue light?"

"Yes, er, and when I walked over and touched it, my hand and the whole of my arm began to tingle."

"You mean like if you had touched a faulty light switch?"

"Yes, just like that."

"Did Arthur touch it?"

"Yes, and he felt it too. It felt as though some unknown force was trapped in the wall itself."

Mike's phone rang. It was Arthur.

"I've looked everywhere outside the stables, Uncle Mike, but there are no signs of disturbances or tyre marks etc. I think we can rule out the kidnap theory."

"OK, Arthur, thanks for calling straight back. I'll be back shortly with the drinks, and Henry's coming to have a look around too. Just sit tight."

Mary and Sam rushed off to the kitchen to make a hot flask for Arthur whilst Henry fired up Google Earth on his computer. He typed in Sha Tin Racecourse and, in less than a minute, they were looking at a map of the racecourse and its surroundings. He made a few prints of the map, to show to Mary and Sam when they returned from the kitchen.

"It all looks so exciting," said Mary, "but I still have reservations about leaving before we find out…"

"I promise it will be all right," replied Mike trying to sound confident. "You mustn't disappoint Sheikh Rashid. Go ahead and take Ivory with you, and we'll follow with Huw and XCalibur as soon as we solve this puzzle!"

Despite his confident manner Sam turned her face away from the others as her eyes filled with tears.

Arthur was glad to see Mike and Henry arrive at the stables. He was by now feeling cold, and was glad to have a hot drink inside him. Henry searched high and low, inside and out, but nothing else came to light. That is, except for the blue glow and the tingling sensation that came from the wall. Henry frowned as he touched the stones. If only they could speak, he thought to himself.

Chapter 4

Merlin

Huw looked at the pieces of paper given to him by Aneurin, and began to read:

Men went to Catraeth (Catterick), swift was their host,
Fresh mead was their feast, and it was poison
Three hundred fighting according to plan
And jubilation there was silence.

Huw soon realised that these were not just random notes recording battle scenes, but were written in the form of poetry. Aneurin was no ordinary scribe. Reading these lines reassured Huw about Aneurin, and he felt that he was the sort of person who wouldn't let him down. Just as these thoughts passed through his mind, there was a rustle in the shrubbery, and Aneurin reappeared with an older man wearing a long scarlet cloak held together at the neckline with a large gold chain embossed with a beautiful Celtic design. The man was tall, with flowing white hair and a long white beard. Huw knew instantly that this was Merlin, and he saw the wisdom of ages reflected in his deep-set eyes. As Huw was about to speak, Merlin held a finger up to his lips, and gestured with his other hand that they should move further away from the edge of the battlefield, so that they could not be overheard.

"Aneurin has already put me in the picture about you," said Merlin.

"And do you understand what's happened?" asked Huw.

"Yes, I do, and I'm not overly surprised."

"You're not?" Huw was taken aback.

"No, because I know from my own experience that time travel is possible. However, it is also a very risky business, and has to be carefully controlled for your own safety."

"But how can it be controlled?"

At this point Merlin reached into a deep pocket in his cloak, and pulled out a bag. The contents of the bag chattered like Huw's teeth often did when out riding on a cold winter's day. Merlin knelt down and emptied some of the bag's contents onto the grass. Huw and Aneurin looked on in awe.

"What are they?" asked Huw.

"Can't you guess?" replied Merlin. "Why, dragon's teeth, of course!"

"But they look so large."

"Perhaps you've never seen a dragon's mouth up close before."

"Well, er…" Huw remembered his encounters with the dragon spirit at Twmp Trelech, but decided to remain silent for now.

As they looked more closely, Huw could see that the teeth had been carved by a craftsman into numbers and letters, and a large hole had been drilled through the top of each one.

"What are the holes for?" asked Huw.

"Let me explain everything," said Merlin. "So listen carefully as you will need to get this absolutely right each time you attempt to time travel."

He then put his hand back into the pocket of his cloak, and produced a finely-made round leather strap, slightly thicker than a pencil.

"Once you decide on your next destination, then you thread the teeth carefully onto the strap, so that they spell out the exact location, date and time of the place you wish to travel to. You then place the strap around XCalibur's neck before you mount him, and hold it as you would the reins. When mounted you must repeat the location and date several times whilst touching the teeth."

"Is this some kind of magic?" asked Huw excitedly.

"Well, er, you might wish to call it that my boy, but whatever you want to call it – the magic force, perhaps – it's produced by the reaction between the dragon's teeth, XCalibur and yourself being a descendant of the Pendragon family."

"But, how did you know that?"

"I see and understand many things Huw, which normal people are unable to comprehend. I suppose it's a special gift I was born with, and the more I use it the stronger it becomes. Now young man, are you ready to return home?"

Huw knew that he must return, but there was so much more he wanted to learn from Merlin.

"I wish I could stay longer," said Huw wistfully.

"But it is very dangerous for you to remain here, with a battle raging."

"Could I come back again please? You see, I was hoping to meet King Arthur."

"Alas, the great king died at the Battle of Camlann in 537 AD. However, if you came back before that time, you might be able to meet him. Now, first things first. We have to get you home safely again. Can you remember everything I told you? Every detail is important!"

"Yes, I remember clearly."

"Good lad, well get ready to remount then."

Merlin gestured to Aneurin to help Huw.

"Make sure you hold the leather strap firmly along with the reins and remember to repeat the exact destination whilst touching the dragon's teeth."

Huw began to repeat the words slowly, and held on like grim death, as he began to feel forces rise within XCalibur. The last words he heard were:

"Good luck Huw... I hope we'll meet again." The words were spoken by Aneurin.

Then he was back in the long dark tunnel.

Chapter 5

Proof from the Past

Arthur was beginning to doze off in the stable, after wondering for
some time if something serious had happened to Huw. His eyelids
drooped and his head fell forward. He fell asleep and began to
dream. He watched as an ambulance pulled up outside the stables,
and two paramedics walked inside with a stretcher. He heard
voices, but something prevented him from going in to help. The
men came out, and carried a boy on the stretcher into the back
of the ambulance. As the ambulance drove away, its blue lights
were flashing. Then Arthur awoke to see the far wall of the stable
throbbing with a pale blue light, which got stronger and stronger
until a hole appeared in the wall, and through the hole leapt Huw
and XCalibur.

Arthur reeled back in shock, and couldn't believe his eyes.

"Where've you been, we've been looking for you for hours... we
thought you'd had a serious accident or something... and how did
you get through that wall?"

"I'm OK," said Huw, calmly dismounting, "and as you can see
so is XCalibur. If I tell you what happened, you won't believe me."

"Try me," said Arthur.

"All right, but first, I need a drink, if you've got anything!"

"You're in luck! Your dad brought a flask of hot tea, and some sandwiches a short while ago. He's worried sick about you. Here, drink this, and tell me what happened."

He handed a mug to Huw, who gulped down the hot sweet tea gratefully, and then took a bite from a ham sandwich.

"Something very strange happened this morning," said Huw in between mouthfuls. "It all began when I took the golden bridle and placed it over XCalibur. Then I began to stroke his blaze, and the next thing I knew, I was hanging on to the reins like grim death. We were flying through a dark tunnel, and when we reached the other end, we were standing on the edge of a battlefield."

"A battlefield!" said Arthur, looking anxiously at Huw as if he had suddenly gone stark raving mad.

"Yes, but luckily for us, we were grabbed by Aneurin, and quickly hidden in some nearby shrubbery."

"Who's Aneurin?"

"Well it seems he was a recorder, making notes of the battle. He was too young to fight himself."

"What battle are we talking about?" said Arthur, sceptically.

"The Battle of Catraeth/Catterick."

"And when did it take place?"

"Around 590 AD."

"What? You must be delirious or something. Did you have a fall from XCalibur? Why did you ride out before I had a chance to get here? You never ride alone, so what possessed you?"

"I've told you what happened Arth, and I'm not delirious or injured in any way. That's exactly what happened. What's more, I've got some proof to show you!"

"Proof? What proof?"

Huw produced the grubby pieces of paper given to him by

Aneurin, and handed them to Arthur, who looked at them very dubiously.

"But these notes could have been written by anyone," said Arthur.

"Could they now, well read them carefully, and I think you might change you mind."

As Arthur began to read, he realised that the words were very moving, and almost poetic, and not just a hurried record of the ebb and flow of battle. It appeared to be written in verses, and took the form of an epic poem. There was a title at the top of the first page, which said *The Gododdin* and, as he read, he realised that the verses described the heroic deeds of 300 warriors of the Gododdin tribe. He was reminded of a film he had seen recently, *The 300 Spartans* which had made a big impression on him.

300 fighting according to plan
And after jubilation there was silence...

Huw could see that Arthur's expression was changing, and there was a look of confusion in his eyes.

"Well, if that hasn't convinced you, then take a look at these," said Huw placing the curiously-shaped objects in Arthur's hand.

"But what are they?"

"Dragon's teeth," said Huw.

"Dragon's what?"

"Teeth."

"But how...?"

"They were given to me by Merlin."

"Merlin the magician?" Arthur was now in a state of total shock and disbelief.

"Merlin explained to me how to use the teeth for time travelling, so that you can choose your exact destination." Huw explained the process in detail, while Arthur listened in amazement.

Arthur was desperate for some excitement and, though he knew just how worried Mike and the others were, he couldn't bring himself to make the phone call. Instead, he sent a text message: "Think I have a lead on Hw wl get bck to u soon." He put his mobile phone back in his bag and pulled out a history book, which Parchy (Mr Padfield) had lent them for their history homework.

"What are you looking up?" asked Huw.

"A list of King Arthur's battles."

"What for?"

"I want to go back in time with you, and meet the king himself," said Arthur.

Huw grinned knowingly. He knew that Arthur wouldn't be able to resist the prospect of time travel, and if it meant meeting King Arthur himself... well... he couldn't resist the thought himself, either.

They scanned the list of battles, and settled on the Battle of Badon 515 AD. They decided to aim for this date, and reorganised the dragon's teeth on the leather strap before placing it around XCalibur's neck. They both mounted the horse, and repeated in unison the date and time of their destination.

Chapter 6

Fantastic Light

A large dark green Range Rover pulling a horse box, both unmarked for security reasons, arrived at Grant Court to pick up Mary, Henry, Sam and Ivory. Soon they were on their way to the Godolphin Stables near Newmarket, where a private jet belonging to Sheikh Rashid was waiting to take them to Hong Kong.

"Is there any news about Huw yet?" asked Sam, looking anxious.

"Not really," said Mary, "but Arthur texted Mike to say he had picked up a lead and was following it, but nothing definite yet."

"How long will it take us to get to Newmarket?"

"About three hours, I should think," said Henry. "We can't travel too fast with Ivory in the horse box. I'll be glad when we've boarded the plane, and secured her in the rear compartment."

"I hope she'll be OK," said Sam.

"'Course she will," replied Henry, reassuringly.

"She'll be well looked after in a separate soundproofed compartment, where she'll be well secured to prevent her moving about, and I'll stay with her as well as her groom Sally throughout the journey to make sure she comes to no harm."

Time passed quickly, and the next thing Sam knew was that they were aboard the plane, and flying on the long journey to Hong

Kong. They each had their own sleeping berths, and Sam was soon fast asleep and dreaming that her friends Huw and Arthur were travelling somewhere in a long dark tunnel. She called out to them, but they seemed not to hear as if they were travelling in a different time to some unknown place.

When she awoke, Sam heard the pilot announcing that in half an hour's time, they would be landing at Hong Kong International Airport, situated on Lantau Island. They would touch down on a private runway from where they would be transported along the airport expressway to a safe residence, a property owned by Sheikh Rashid.

Soon they had left the airport behind, and were travelling quickly along the expressway in an easterly direction, towards Hong Kong. The view from the windows of the dark green unmarked Range Rover was unlike anything Sam had ever seen. The route followed a causeway linking small islands together, and eventually to the mainland. There seemed to be large stretches of water everywhere with wooded hills sweeping down to the sea. The hills were dotted with buildings large and small, some old and some new, and all seeming to reflect the bright light of the early morning sun as it rose in the eastern sky.

The road ahead began to rise as they swept passed the Sha Tin Racecourse, and soon they were driving through wooded hills towards their destination. Qing, the chauffeur, eventually stopped outside some large ornamental gates supported by huge thick pillars. He lowered his window, and spoke into a microphone hidden in a small recess in the right hand pillar and, a few seconds later, the gates began to open. Once through the gates, the road traversed a curved bridge with seventeen arches, and Sam gasped at the sight before her. The bridge crossed over a large lake on the other side of which was a small island. Qing told them that this was known as the Island of the Dragon King. The road reached the end of the bridge, skirted the island on which stood several buildings, and then mounted another bridge, this time with 27 archways, at the far end of which rose a hill covered in pine woodlands. At the top of the hill stood a magnificent house built in traditional Chinese style. It must have been a palace once thought Sam, and she felt a tingle of excitement at the prospect of staying in this magical place for the next few weeks.

As Sam stepped out of the car, she looked up in awe at the colourful façade of the main building. It was built in the style of a pavilion, with curved roofs overhanging brightly coloured walls and terraces boldly decorated in gold, blue, red, and green, filled with delicate pictures of flowers and trees. The front steps led up to a grand entrance framed with pillars, and there stood the house keeper, Madame Wang Li, and her daughter, Cha Li. Cha Li raced down the steps to greet Sam.

"Welcome to Hong Kong," she said giving Sam a flashing smile. "I'm sure you're going to be very happy here."

"Thank you," replied Sam. "It's so beautiful."

"Come in, come in," said Madame Wang Li warmly. "Let's get you settled in, and then Cha Li can show you around the estate. There's a lot to see, but first we must give you some refreshments after your long journey."

Two Chinese porters helped Sam and Mary with their suitcases and bags, and a stable boy accompanied Henry to the horsebox, from where they took Ivory to the stable block behind the main pavilion.

As they crossed the large entrance hall leading to the grand central staircase, Sam was struck by the shimmering light entering through the tall windows.

"I've never seen such a magical light before," she said, gazing at the flickering shadows on the walls and ceiling.

"That's why the house is called Fantastic Light," said Cha Li. "Sheikh Rashid was so enchanted by it that he renamed the house after the horse called Fantastic Light which won the Hong Kong World Championship in 2000."

"He must have been a wonderful horse!"

"Yes, he was, and he had a champion jockey too!"

"Who was that?" asked Sam.

"Why, Frankie Dettori, of course!"

"Of course," replied Sam, trying to sound knowledgeable. "So what was the original name of the house?"

"My mother told me it was Mana, which means magic."

"What a magical place it is," said Sam. "This is going to be a very special time, I can feel it in my bones."

They climbed the stairs and followed a long corridor until they reached two doors, side by side.

"The blue door is mine," said Cha Li, "and the red one is yours. If you need anything at any time, you know where to find me. Now come on, let's get you unpacked, then you can have a good rest before dinner. Don't worry if you fall asleep, I'll give you a call one hour beforehand, so you'll have plenty of time to get ready."

"Thank you so much," said Sam. "I'm really bushed after the long journey."

*

At dinner that evening, the conversation centred on two things – Huw's strange disappearance, and Sheikh Rashid's arrival the next day.

"Is there any more news about Huw?" asked Sam.

"Nothing more yet," replied Henry, "but Mike has promised to text me as soon as they have a lead. There's a full-scale search going on around the stables, and I'm sure something will turn up soon." Henry tried to sound as positive as he could for Sam's sake, but inwardly he was fearing the worst.

"Henry's right," said Mary adding her support. "Now let's talk about something exciting instead. Sheikh Rashid is arriving tomorrow, and we must be ready to welcome him after his long journey from Dubai."

"I can't wait to meet Prince Ahmed and Princess Sheba again," said Sam.

"Oh yes, and don't forget you have a new friend now to introduce them to." Mary smiled and looked towards Cha Li.

"It's going to be so exciting," said Sam reaching out to take hold of Cha Li's hand. "I can't wait for tomorrow to come!"

Cha Li whispered something in Sam's ear.

"Oh, and Mum could I have permission to visit the Ten Thousand Buddhas Monastery early tomorrow morning? Cha Li has offered to take me there. It's not very far away, and we'll be back well before noon when Sheikh Rashid is due to arrive!"

Mary looked towards Madame Wang Li, who nodded in agreement. "It will be quite safe," she said, "and I will arrange for the chauffeur Qing to take them there, and see that they come to no harm."

Sam glanced at Cha Li and smiled contentedly.

*

Early the next morning, chauffeur Qing picked them up at the main entrance, and soon they were crossing the lake via the arched bridges and heading towards a wooded hill on the other side of the water.

"That's where we're heading," said Cha Li, pointing towards a temple-like building standing on top of the hill.

"Is that the monastery?" asked Sam.

"Yes, it's famous throughout China, and one of the oldest shrines to Buddha."

"And are there really 10,000 statues there?" asked Sam excitedly.

"They say there are now more than 14,000," replied Cha Li, "but its name hasn't changed. There are large life-size statues outside and smaller ones inside."

When they arrived at the monastery, Qing parked the Range Rover and told them that he would wait for them there. He felt sure that they would be safe inside, and they had their mobile phones should they need to call him. He gave them the entrance fees, and told them to take care when climbing the steps inside.

Once inside, Sam gazed in wonder at the ruby lipped, life-size golden Buddhas lining the steep path leading up to the temple.

"Look," said Cha Li, pointing towards a Buddha sitting astride a giant white elephant, and another on top of a large dog.

"I've never seen anything like this before," said Sam, feeling dwarfed by the giant elephant.

"These statues were made to show how much Buddha cared for animals," said Cha Li. "Both domestic and in the wild!"

At the centre of the monastery stood a bright red pagoda-style building with nine storeys. They climbed the stairs inside, each level lined with shelves of golden Buddhas, until they reached the top, 200 steps later. From there they could see the whole layout of the monastery down below, and beyond that the shimmering lake and the Fantastic Light house in the distance. They descended the steps carefully until they were back at the entrance to the pagoda. Sam noticed there were two red dragon statues guarding the entrance, one of each side.

"I didn't really notice those when we entered," said Sam.

"No, I think you were looking up at the time," said Cha Li. "These are known as the guardians of the temple, and there are various stories about those brave enough to put their hands in a dragon's mouth. Some say they have had vivid dreams, and even had their hands bitten off. So most people give them a wide berth."

Sam had a sudden urge to put her hand into one of the dragons' open mouths, and before Cha Li could say anything, she plunged her hand in. As she touched the dragon's teeth, she felt a strange tingling sensation, her eyes closed, and she had a strange image of Huw and XCalibur standing on the edge of a battlefield. She instinctively knew that Huw was in grave danger, and she felt powerless to help him.

She pulled her hand out of the dragon's mouth, looked at Cha Li in alarm, and gasped. For a moment it looked as though Sam was going to faint, but Cha Li put her arm around her and gently steered her in the direction of a Chinese teahouse close by.

Chapter 7

The Iron Horse

For the first time in his life, Arthur was really scared. He clung on to Huw's waist as they rushed back through the space tunnel.

"Hold on tight," said Huw, as XCalibur sped through the tunnel with his head thrust forward as he strained on the leash.

"What's happening?" cried Arthur through clenched teeth, as he tried hard to keep his mouth shut against the force of the wind.

It was Huw's turn to smile, although he himself felt far from confident. The intensity of the blue light increased as they neared the end of the tunnel, and the sheer power of the wind took their breath away. Then, suddenly, the wind dropped and they were at the end of the tunnel and had landed on yet another battlefield. But this time they were in the thick of it! Huw felt a surge of anxiety as he realized how fiercely the fighting was raging all around them, and how vulnerable they were as swords clashed on shields. The din was almost unbearable as swordsmen and horses fell in the heat of battle.

Huw looked up and saw Merlin standing on a hillock at the edge of the battlefield, with his arms held high above his head. He seemed to be speaking to the clouds overhead, but his words were drowned by the relentless noise. Then something miraculous happened, and Huw felt himself being metamorphosed into a young warrior. He looked down to see himself encased in armour, and he held a sword in his right hand.

"This is incredible!" shouted Arthur behind him, as he too experienced the same change. "But what about XCalibur? He's just as vulnerable as we are if not more so!"

"Look," shouted Huw nodding his head downward. "Something's happening to XCalibur too. This is awesome!"

Arthur felt the horse's back changing beneath him. It was expanding and becoming more rigid, yet there was no creaking or groaning which you might expect if a horse made of flesh and blood was changing into an iron horse. There were gasps of amazement from the horsemen and foot soldiers who were fighting around them. No-one had ever witnessed a transformation like this before and, for a few seconds, the fighting stopped and everyone stood there gaping. All the other horses stood still, snorting and wheezing with clouds of hot breath bursting from their open mouths and flaring nostrils. XCalibur now looked like the framework of a sculptor's bronze before the clay was laid on. A metal skeleton.

XCalibur, the iron horse, stood there majestically at the centre of a small circle which had opened up at the epicentre of the battle. Inside the circle all was calm, just as it is in the eye of a hurricane.

The silence was broken when a strong arm, protected in amour, reached out and grasped the top end of XCalibur's blaze which was now the handle of a great broadsword.

"Excalibur I think!" cried the owner of the strong arm, flourishing the sword as if he was holding a light sabre on the film set of *Star Wars*. The sword shone with a powerful light and temporarily blinded the enemy so that XCalibur, Huw and Arthur were able to forge a path through the bewildered soldiers in the enemy's ranks.

"Look," shouted Huw, "it must be King Arthur. There's a dragon standard, and a royal dragon crest on his coat of armour!"

"Don't look round now," said Arthur in Huw's ear. "But we've also got an escort of knights behind us."

The band of knights rode past them and formed a wedge which drove through the enemy ranks. Enemy foot soldiers thrust long pikes towards them, but King Arthur wielded Excalibur from one flank to the other shattering the pikes into splinters. XCalibur, Huw and Arthur were unaffected by swords, pikes and arrows which failed to penetrate their armour. Gradually they pushed the enemy back towards a ridge where their leader stood surveying the ebb and flow of the battle. He was a fine figure of a man, with flowing red hair and beard.

"Who is it?" shouted Huw.

"It's Hengist!" cried on of the leading knights. "If we can capture him then the battle will be over."

"Hold your horses!" commanded King Arthur. "He is a fierce warrior and leader of his men. Therefore it should fall to me to face him in a one-to-one combat."

"But, sire," called out the knights in unison, "the risk is too high."

"It's already been foretold," said the king. "Merlin told me this morning, before the battle commenced, and I knew it would be so. These days you have to earn your kingship; there is no other way and even if there was, I would not want it. Fear not good knights, for I have the trusted Excalibur in my hand, and I shall give a good account of myself."

The knights reluctantly agreed, and the wedge opened up for the king to ride through and call out a challenge to Hengist the Red. Hengist refused to mount up, and demanded that King Arthur dismount and fight him on foot. He knew he would be no match for the king on horseback, and sought to gain the advantage in hand-to-hand combat. He was also cunning and charged at King Arthur before he had dismounted properly. It was a cowardly act, but the king was prepared and used his shield to deflect the first blow.

"I don't like the sly grin on Hengist's face," said Huw as they positioned themselves amongst the ranks of the knights for protection.

"Fear not young warrior," replied Sir Lancelot. "The king is very alert when it comes to facing the Saxons in battle."

"But how can he guess what Hengist will do next if he doesn't fight fairly?"

"Just watch his eyes," said Lancelot.

Huw looked first at Hengist, whose eyes were furtive and nervous, glancing from left to right in search of some devious way to gain an unfair advantage. King Arthur's eyes were like steel and did not waver. He looked straight at Hengist's eyes and waited for the slightest hint of movement.

Hengist gave a slight nod of the head, and one of his warriors threw a lance in his direction.

"Look out," cried Huw. "He's going to charge the king!"

As Hengist lunged forward with the lance, King Arthur moved deftly to one side, and sliced the lance in two with Excalibur. Only two sweeps of the sword were necessary for as Hengist plunged forward with the broken lance the king drove the blade into his chest. The chain mail he wore was no match for the flashing sword which moved like lightning in King Arthur's hand. The fight was over and the battle was won; Hengist's warriors threw down their arms and withdrew from the scene of conflict.

Chapter 8

Historical Clues

Huw's father Mike returned to the stables on Saturday evening, hoping that Arthur had found Huw and XCalibur, or that at least he might have some good news. As he approached the stable block he noticed that one of the doors was open, but there was no sign of life.

"Arthur!" he called, his voice beginning to show real signs of anxiety. "This is not a joke any longer, what on earth's going on?"

As he entered XCalibur's stable he saw some of Arthur's belongings on the floor, but there was no sign of life. He decided to look in the other stables to see if Arthur had borrowed one of the other horses so that he could ride out in search of Huw. But all the other horses were secure. Harry, one of the older stable boys, came running up as he had heard Mike calling out.

"Is everything alright Mr Pendry?" he asked breathlessly.

"If I'm honest with you Harry, I'm beginning to get really worried. First, Huw went missing, with XCalibur, and now Arthur's missing too."

"Let's have another look around XCalibur's stable," said Harry trying to allay some of Mike's fears. "We might find something that'll help."

"All right," said Mike without much conviction, and they both began to search more thoroughly.

"Look!" said Harry, "have you noticed that the stones on the external wall are stained with a strange blue colour!"

Mike frowned and then reached out and touched the wall. He withdrew his hand quickly, as if he had just had an electric shock.

"That's odd," he said, "it's as if the wall is alive." Harry touched the stones too, and had the same reaction.

"Look," said Harry, "the blue stain is shaped like a large circle, as if it's been hit by a large paint ball."

Mike stared at the blue-tinged stones. What had happened to them, he wondered? He looked at his fingers, but they were not stained in any way, so it wasn't paint.

"It's not paint," said Mike.

"Then what on earth is it?!" Harry gazed at the large circle which was about the size of a London Underground tunnel. He imagined a train disappearing through the wall, as if he was watching a movie on TV. He looked down and then saw a crumpled piece of paper at the base of the wall.

"What's this?" remarked Harry, as he unfolded the piece of paper and tried to smooth it out on a bench at the side of the stable. Mike crossed over, and they both stared at the handwritten words scrawled on the parchment...

Where his weapons struck there was no return blow,
He was unwavering in his ferocity...

At the bottom of the page, they could just make out a name.

"What does it say?" asked Harry, looking confused.

"It looks like An... An... Aneurin," said Mike.

"Who's he?"

"Dunno yet… but maybe we can find out!"

"This paper…"

"Parchment," said Mike.

"Is that what it is? Looks really old."

"It is very old!"

"How old?"

"One thousand five hundred years… maybe."

"But how do you know that?"

"Educated guess," said Mike, thinking about the books at home which Parchy (Mr Padfield) had lent Huw for his project on battles in the fifth and sixth centuries.

"Do you think Huw dropped it?"

"It's a possibility."

"But why there, against the wall?"

"Dunno."

Mike made a quick decision, walked determinedly back to the blue wall, and thrust his hand firmly against it. This time, his arm disappeared up to the elbow.

"What the blazes?" he cried out.

Harry rushed across from the bench, and grasped Mike around the waist, as it looked as if he was about to be sucked through the wall by some unknown force. Harry tugged hard, and they both fell backwards as Mike's arm was released by the vice-like grip of the blue stones. They were both shaken, but neither was badly hurt. As Harry scrambled to his feet, a shaft of moonlight shone through a window in the front wall of the stable near the door. Harry spotted something partly hidden beneath a pile of hay in the corner. The moonlight picked out an image of the silver blade of a sword emblazoned on the corner of a book. Mike rose to his feet as Harry plucked the book from beneath the hay.

"Looks like one of the books you mentioned," said Harry, as he handed it over to Mike.

"*King Arthur...* by John Matthews," said Mike as he read the beautifully illustrated cover, "and if I'm not mistaken this sword must be Excalibur."

He opened the cover to find the owner's name written in the top right-hand corner: Charles Padfield, History Department, Newent School.

"It's Parchy's all right," he said, brushing off bits of hay that were trapped beneath the cover. "It's a good thing he's not here to see it like this."

"Perhaps it fell there by accident," suggested Harry trying to defuse the situation. "Something unexpected may have happened and the book toppled off the bench."

"Yes, we'd better give them the benefit of the doubt, I suppose," Mike replied, stifling his growing anger and frustration.

"There's a bookmark sticking out from one of the pages."

"So there is," said Mike opening the book at the relevant page...

The Battle of Badon 515 AD was written at the top of the page, and there followed a detailed account of the ebb and flow of the battle which involved King Arthur and many of his knights.

"I still don't understand any of this," said Mike. "All this history is getting us nowhere fast. There's only one thing for it now. I'm going to call in the police. This whole business is becoming too serious, and I'm very worried about the boys."

"You're right, sir. Shall I dial 999?"

"No thanks Harry, leave it to me. I've got a direct line to Detective Chief Inspector Mabon. He'll be just the man for this job."

Chapter 9

The Coded Messages

Once Sam had returned safely to Fantastic Light she soon recovered from her fright at the Ten Thousand Buddhas Monastery.

Cha Li knocked on her bedroom door and entered to tell Sam that Sheikh Rashid and the Dubai Royal family had arrived, and asked whether she was up to going downstairs to greet them.

"Wouldn't miss it for the world!" said Sam, and leapt out of bed as if nothing untoward had happened. They ran down the great staircase and arrived in the hall just as Madame Wang Li was welcoming the royal guests at the main entrance. Sam curtsied to Sheikh Rashid before giving Princess Sheba a big hug and then introducing everyone to Cha Li.

"It's so good to see you all again," said Sam. "Come on Sheba, let me help you with your bags upstairs. I've got so much to tell you about what's happened since we last met."

"I'll help too," said Cha Li, and Henry was on hand to assist Sheikh Rashid and Ahmed with some extra help from Ping and Pong, the house porters.

Once in Prince Ahmed's bedroom, Henry told him about the mysterious disappearance of Huw, Arthur and XCalibur from the Grant Court stables. Mike had telephoned Henry early that morning with the latest news.

"Had they all disappeared at the same time?" asked Ahmed with a look of genuine concern on his face.

"No, that's the strange part of the whole thing," replied Henry. "Huw and XCalibur went missing first. Arthur remained at the stables while everyone else was out searching. Then sometime later Arthur disappeared too."

"It sounds like one of those mysterious stories from *The Arabian Nights*," said Ahmed.

"Yes, but this is happening NOW."

"What can we do to help?" asked Ahmed.

"Perhaps we'd better tell Sam and Sheba," replied Henry, "so that they'll be prepared before we have dinner with Sheikh Rashid this evening. It wouldn't be right to alarm them too much on their first day in Hong Kong, would it?"

"No, you're absolutely right," said Ahmed. "Let's go along to Sam's room, and put them in the picture right away!"

They walked quickly along the long corridor until they reached the girls' quarters. A yellow post-it note was stuck on one of the doors: "Sheba was eager to visit the Ten Thousand Buddhas Monastery before dinner. Don't worry, Madame Wang Li gave me permission and we've taken a taxi. See you later, love Sam!"

"Oh Lord," said Henry, "I hope they know what they're doing!"

*

Inside the teahouse was divided into alcoves, separated by glass partitions which offered some degree of privacy from the other customers. Cha Li ordered some Chinese tea, and hoped that Sam would find it very refreshing. As they waited for their order, Cha Li noticed a group of men huddled in the far corner – they seemed to be speaking in whispers and looking around nervously whenever someone entered the teahouse.

"What is it?" asked Sam, still feeling strange.

"I'm not sure yet," replied Cha Li holding her finger up to her lips and making a quiet 'shhh' sound. They all leant forward across the table and put their heads together.

"Don't look now, but the men in the far corner seem to be behaving strangely and in a covert manner. It might be my imagination, but I think they're up to something."

"Let's try to act normally," whispered Sam as the waiter brought their tea and a bowl of Chinese crackers for them to share. "Let's play 'make a picture'," she said, taking a sheet from the small note book she carried in her bag. She drew a line on the page and then passed it to the person sitting next to her, and so it went around the table with each one adding a new line. This helped to focus their attention away from the men in the corner. That is, with the exception of Cha Li, who occasionally glanced at the group from the corner of her eye, whilst seeming to drink from her cup. She noticed that not all the men were Chinese, although they seemed to be dressed in similar black shirts and trousers, and each one had a black tattoo on the back of his right hand, but she was too far away to make a clear mental image of it.

As she struggled to identify the tattoo, the men rose and left the teahouse silently. Cha Li looked across to the place where they had been sitting, and noticed something lying on the floor beneath one of the tables. She waited a few moments to ensure that none of the men returned, and then crossed over to pick up the object which turned out to be four sheets of paper stapled together.

"What is it?" asked Sam.

"They dropped this on the floor before they left," said Cha Li.

"Can you make sense of it?"

"No," said Cha Li, "it's written in some kind of coded language."

"Is each page the same?"

"They're all coded, but there seems to be a different code on each page."

Sam and Sheba studied the pages closely, but neither of them could make any immediate sense of the words. However, there was one thing that stood out at the top of each page. It was a picture of a cobra's head.

"That's it!" said Cha Li excitedly. "That's the same image I saw on the man's right hand."

"You mean the tattoo?" asked Sam.

"Yes, the tattoo, that's definitely what I saw, and I think each of the men had the same tattoo on the back of his right hand."

"I can tell you something else too," said Sheba, who was much more familiar with snakes than the others.

"What's that?"

"The cobra is ready to strike!"

"I think we'd better return to the safe residence," said Sam, "and give ourselves some time to think things over calmly. There might not be anything sinister in all this, but those men looked very nervous when they left."

"I agree," said Cha Li, "but we'd better be on our guard when we leave the teahouse. Let me go first, as I know this district well, but follow close behind me and keep your eyes peeled!"

As soon as they left the teahouse, Cha Li noticed two men hiding in a doorway across the street. She whispered to the others to follow

First Coded Message.

HONG KONG

SHA-TIN RACE COURSE
H.K. CHALLENGE GOLD CUP
HACK INTO RACE MEETING
COMPUTER SYSTEM — TRANSFER
ALL BETTING MONEY INTO
OUR SECRET CODED ACCOUNT
— ALSO GO TO 10,000
BUDDHAS MONASTERY AND
REMOVE STATUE OF FOUNDING
MONK COVERED IN GOLD LEAF
ENCLOSED IN GLASS CASE.

Second Coded Message.

	R	G	A	M	F	G	A	H
G	H	R	S	N	Q	X	L	T R D T L —
Q	D	L	N	U	D	R	D	U D Q A K
R	G	A	M	F	A	Q	N	M Y D Y H M D
U	D	R	R	D	K	R	—	A K R N
R	A	M	B	A	K	S	G	Q D D B N K N
T	Q	B	D	Q	A	L	H	B R A M C
B	D	K	A	C	N	M	V	A K D.
I	A	C	D	A	T	C	C	G A S D L O K D
S	U	N	K	A	Q	F	D	I A C D
A	T	C	C	G	A	R	S	A S T D R N M D
Q	D	B	K	H	M	H	M	F, N M D R D A
S	D	C.	S	A	J	D	A	K K A A N U D
S	Q	D	A	R	T	G	D	R S N R D B Q
D	S	G	H	C	D	N	T	S.

54

Third Coded Message.

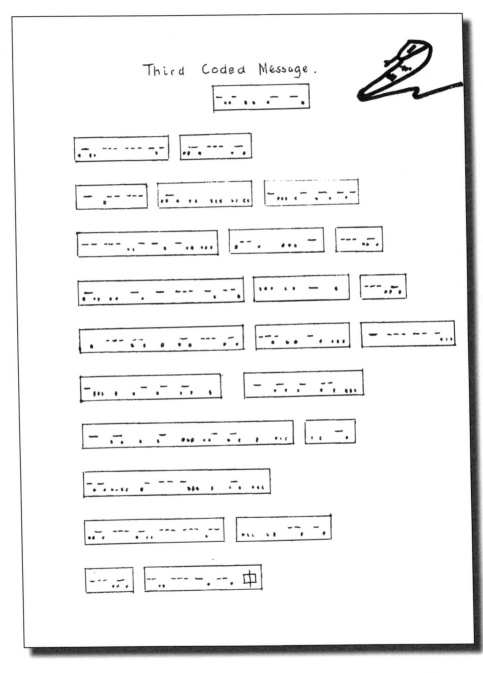

her to the next corner and then, once into the next street, to run fast into an alleyway. Cha Li led the way as they turned this way and that, through a maze of narrow alleys until she eventually stopped outside a tall three-storey town house. Sam and Sheba looked up in surprise as Cha Li opened the front door and hustled them quickly inside.

"Where on earth are we?" asked Sam.

"Don't worry," replied Cha Li. "We're safe now. This is my friend's house. There's no way they'll find us here!"

"Thank goodness for that," said Sheba. "I thought I was pretty fit, but I'm really out of breath, and I was afraid they were close behind."

Cha Li held her finger up to her lips, and beckoned to Sam and Sheba to sit on the bottom stair of a fairly steep staircase leading up to the first floor. She slowly opened the front door and peered gingerly out into the alleyway. All was quiet, and there were no sounds of men's voices or shoes clattering on the cobbles. She closed the door quietly, and locked and bolted if before leading the way upstairs.

Chapter 10

King Arthur and Merlin

Following the Battle of Badon in 515 AD, Huw, Arthur and XCalibur watched the clearing operation take place from the edge of the battlefield. The knights organised teams of soldiers to help carry the dead and the wounded from the scene of battle. The sight was terrifying for all those looking on, especially Huw and Arthur, who had never witnessed anything like this in real life before, only on their PlayStation games.

"I don't think I ever want to play one of those war games ever again," said Huw feeling sick.

"It's a horrible sight," agreed Arthur. "You wonder why anyone would want to engage in anything like this – it's so senseless."

Much time was devoted to caring for those who were dying and seriously wounded, and the knights and soldiers worked tirelessly to ensure that no soldier was overlooked. The casualties were taken to large tents that had been set up nearby well before the battle commenced. Healers and carers were present to look after those who were injured. There were separate tents for injured horses, with animal carers in attendance. The whole area was like a large military field hospital.

Once the fallen had been safely gathered in, then the knights and infantrymen were able to rest. King Arthur and his royal knights rested in a large red tent, and discussed the events of the battle, including the arrival of Huw, Arthur and the iron horse. The latter was the subject of much conversation, as no-one had ever witnessed anything like it before. King Arthur asked for the boys to be called into the royal tent, and that XCalibur be well looked after in the temporary canvas stables.

When Huw and Arthur were ushered in, they bowed their heads as a mark of respect for the king.

"It's a great honour to meet you, sire," said Huw. "I never in my wildest dreams thought that this could ever happen."

"Please, come along and sit here alongside me, and next to Merlin and my trusted knights. You have both been very brave today, and this must have been quite an ordeal for you to witness a battle like this for the first time. It's difficult enough for us to bear, and we are battle-hardened soldiers."

Merlin interjected, "With your permission, sire, may I relate to you what happened before today, so that you will understand why the boys are here?"

"Please go ahead," said the king.

Merlin told of his earlier encounter with Huw and XCalibur and of their meeting with Aneurin, although the Battle of Catraeth (Catterick) had not yet taken place in real time. Merlin told how he had given Huw a collection of dragons' teeth with magical properties so that he could return safely to the future through the time portal. King Arthur was astonished to hear Merlin's tale.

"You mean you've come here from the future?!"

"Yes, sire," replied Huw.

"But, how did this happen in the first place?"

Huw explained how he had placed the golden bridle around

XCalibur's neck, and how he had then found himself travelling through a tunnel which took him back in time.

"But this is unbelievable," said the king, sounding somewhat sceptical.

"I can assure you it's true," said Merlin. "I, too, found it hard to believe at first, but I know from my own past experiences that these things can happen when the circumstances are right."

"But what exactly were these special circumstances?"

"Well, sire, it would seem that when young Huw placed the medallion he had found at the burial mound back on the golden bridle which had belonged to your cousin Culhwch, this triggered off a chain of events. Huw then placed the bridle around the neck of XCalibur, and this set the time clock ticking. It suggests to me that there is a genetic connection between XCalibur and Culhwch's horse."

"You mean XCalibur is descended from..."

"Yes, sire."

The king turned towards Huw and said, "Well young man, and what is the name of XCalibur's mother?"

"Ivory, sire," replied Huw nervously.

"So why is he jet black?"

"His father is called Ebony, sire, an Arab thoroughbred belonging to Sheikh Rashid of Dubai."

"Dubai! And where on earth is that?"

"In the Middle East, sire," interjected Merlin much to Huw's relief, "and Sheikh Rashid is a renowned nobleman of the 21st century who has a great love of horses."

"Well," said the king, "this is indeed a remarkable discovery. It looks like our horses are related, as well as ourselves. I've no doubt we're all part of one big family, and as long as you are with us you will be treated as royalty! Gentlemen, it is my great pleasure," continued the king now addressing the entire assembly, "to introduce you all to Prince Huw, Prince Arthur, and the royal colt, XCalibur!"

A great cheer arose from the knights and everyone present in the royal tent. The king beamed and placed a hand on each boy's shoulder as he drew them to his side, while Merlin gathered up XCalibur's reins and whispered something in his ear. Whatever it was Merlin said, the young colt held his head high and remained completely calm during the loud and prolonged cheering.

"Now my gallant knights," proclaimed the king, "I would like you Cei (Kay), Bedwyr (Bedivere) Gwalchmai (Gawain), and Gwrhur to take the young princes to their sleeping quarters for tonight as I know they must be exhausted, and please remain on guard there until daybreak. Meanwhile Merlin, would you please take XCalibur to the field stables, and secure him for the night. Tomorrow we will take stock of the situation, and prepare for our next encounter with those who threaten our homeland. Goodnight gentlemen!"

Chapter 11

Mabon
examines the evidence

"Congratulations on your promotion to detective chief inspector," Mike said to Richard Mabon as he shook his hand warmly, "and welcome back to Grant Court. Unfortunately, the news is not good, and I'm very grateful to you for coming so quickly."

"Thanks for your warm welcome, but I didn't like the sound of what you told me on the phone, bearing in mind what's happened to the boys in the past, and I decided to come right away. If you and Harry will fill me in about exactly what you've found so far, then I can take the investigation from there. It would probably be best if you both went about your work, as I know you will have lots to do in the other stables. I have already sent for forensics, so we will need to cordon off the stable, and begin our search inside."

Mike and Harry related what they had already found and then went about their business. Mabon began to scrutinise the inside of the stable thoroughly. There were three things that needed closer examination: the blue stained wall, the grubby papers signed by Aneurin, and the open history book. As he began his investigation, two police constables arrived and began to cordon off the stable. They were quickly followed by two forensic officers and an archivist from the National Museum of Wales in Cardiff. One of the forensic team was a photographer, and he set up his equipment with a powerful light shining on the wall. Mabon and the photographer studied the wall together.

"The blue stained circle seems to show that particles from the atmosphere appear to have crystallised on the wall," said the photographer.

"Yes," said Mabon, "it's as if the stones in the wall appear to have melted in some great heat force which turned the stones into blue glass."

"That's possible," said the second forensic officer, "if the stone contained high quantities of silica and quartz, then it could metamorphose into glass. But what would produce such an intense heat in the first place?"

"That's what we're here to find out," said Mabon. "Take as many pictures as you can, and magnify them as much as possible. We'll also need samples from the wall to take back for analysis in the labs."

The archivist was meanwhile studying the grubby papers signed by Aneurin.

"What do you make of these?" asked Mabon.

"Well, they're very old, that's certain."

"How old?"

"If I had to hazard a guess before carrying out carbon dating, I would say 1,500 years."

"Phew," gasped Mabon, "but how did they come to be here?"

"That's a good question, unless they were stolen from the National Library in Aberystwyth, but I haven't heard of any such theft having taken place. With your permission, sir, I would like to take these back to the museum for further tests."

"Of course, but be aware of the high security risk involved."

"Yes, sir, I will ask the photographer from forensics to copy them first as a precaution, but I will not let them out of my sight after I leave."

"Good man, but before you go, could we talk about the history book which was found here. It's possible that the boys were reading it before they disappeared, and it was found open on the page relating to the Battle of Badon in 515 AD."

The archivist studied the book, and looked at the owner's name written inside the cover. "It looks like Mr Padfield's book, sir. I believe he's the history teacher at the local school."

"That's correct."

"Then, I think I would be inclined to speak with him directly, sir, as he would be the best person to throw more light on this than anyone else."

"You're right," said Mabon. "Leave that to me then, and you do your best with the ancient papers."

"Right, sir, I'm on my way, and I'll get back to you soon."

*

"Can you confirm that this book belongs to you, Mr Padfield?" asked DCI Mabon.

"I certainly can," replied the head of the history department at Newent School, "and I lent the book to Huw and Arthur Pendry last week for a history project they were working on, which covered the Arthurian period in early mediaeval history. But how has the book come into your possession, chief inspector. Have they lost it?"

"Not exactly Mr Padfield, it's much worse than that. You see,

Huw and Arthur and the young colt XCalibur have gone missing from the Grant Court stables, and we are greatly concerned about their safety."

"Good heavens, you mean they might have been kidnapped?"

"Well, that's one possibility, but we've discovered some strange clues at XCalibur's stable which we're investigating right now, ones which are very puzzling to say the least."

"What sort of things? Is there anything I can help you with?"

"I was hoping you might say that," said Mabon showing Mr Padfield the copies of the grubby papers found at the scene. "As you can see these are photocopies of some papers found in the stable – forensics have the originals."

"But this is astonishing. These are copies of an epic poem called *Y Gododdin* written by Aneurin, and are recognised by experts as a detailed record of the Battle of Catraeth [Catterick] in 590 AD. The only copy of this poem that I am aware of is kept in the National Library. How on earth did this turn up in the stable?"

"That's exactly what we're trying to find out," said Mabon, "and if they are genuine, then how did the boys get hold of them?"

"Perhaps they went back in time," said Mr Padfield with a broad grin on his face. "They may have borrowed *Dr Who*'s tardis – now there's a thought!"

Mabon was deep in thought.

"What is it?" said Mr Padfield.

"We found something else at the stable."

"What was that?"

"One of the stone walls had metamorphosed into blue glass due to great heat, and looked like a huge circle on the wall, almost like the entrance to a tunnel."

"What, are you serious?"

"Deadly serious! And not only that, when Mike Pendry pushed his arm against the wall, it disappeared up to the elbow, and seemed to be sucking him in. If it hadn't been for the stable lad Harry, I think he would have gone right through the wall."

"But that's impossible," said Mr Padfield who wasn't grinning any longer, "I know I mentioned time travel a few moments ago, but I was only joking, and everyone knows that *Dr Who* and the tardis are only make believe."

"Well, that's what I thought before all this began, but now I'm not so certain."

Mr Padfield looked completely baffled.

"So far we haven't found any trace of either Huw or Arthur outside the stable. There are no tracks or footprints leading anywhere, which in normal circumstances we would expect to find. So the only conclusion I can reach is that they disappeared inside the stable."

DCI Mabon's mobile phone rang. He listened intently. "You're quite sure about that? Thank you. I'll talk to you again later as soon as I leave here."

"What is it?" asked Mr Padfield.

"Forensics have confirmed that the papers signed by Aneurin have been carbon dated to 590 AD which means that they are the originals."

Mr Padfield gasped in disbelief. "Then the papers in the National Library are…"

"Copies, yes, there can be no doubt that these are the originals which means that someone brought them to the stable."

"From 590 AD! Then someone must have travelled through time for that to happen!"

"There's no other possible explanation," replied Mabon, looking far from convinced that this was a credible explanation. But, right now, it was the only one they had.

Chapter 12

Detective Chief Inspector Chan Arrives

"I'm getting a bit concerned about the girls," said Mary. "It will soon be time for lunch and there's no sign of them yet. It's not like Sam to leave it so long without phoning. I've tried calling her mobile, but it's switched off."

"They'll be fine," said Henry reassuringly, as he put on a clean shirt and brushed his hair. "I expect they've lost count of time at the monastery, and don't forget there's a lot of Buddhas to see in that place – 10,000 if I remember correctly." He was grinning at himself in the mirror.

Mary looked across at Henry and smiled. He always seemed to say the right thing when he knew she was worried.

The bedroom phone rang, and Henry picked up the receiver. It was Madame Wang Li. He repeated her words for Mary's benefit.

"You've had a call from Cha Li. Yes, I understand, there's been an incident and the girls have taken refuge in a friend's house. Right, we'll come downstairs right away, and you can tell us the full story."

Henry hung up, took Mary's hand, and together they left their bedroom and headed quickly downstairs. After listening to the full story from Madame Wang Li, Henry was quite definite about what they should do. "There's something really sinister about this, and I've no doubt we should call in the police. We can't take risks when it comes to the girls' safety."

"I totally agree," said Madame Wang Li. "I suggest we put a call through to DCI Dong Chan. He's a close friend of the family and one of the best in the Hong Kong Special Investigations Squad. I keep his direct line number in my desk drawer." She opened the drawer and flipped through the pages until she came to the C entries, and there he was, at the top of the page. Luck was with them, and the inspector answered right away. "He's coming straight over," said Madame Wang Li, much to Mary's relief. "He'll be here in ten minutes."

Madame Wang Li introduced DCI Chan to Mary and Henry before they all sat down in the large lounge adjoining the hallway. He was younger than Mary had expected, short and stocky, with dark brown eyes which looked very alert. Mary noticed that he looked straight at Madame Wang Li, as she told him about Cha Li's phone call, and his concentration never wavered for an instant.

"Well," he said confidently, "Cha Li has once again shown remarkable maturity under duress, and she has absolutely done the right thing."

"Oh, I do so agree," said Mary, "as long as they don't venture out again before help arrives."

"Have no fears," said the inspector, "I have already sent a couple of undercover officers into the area, just in case their pursuers are loitering in the vicinity. I'm expecting a call from them at any moment to let me know that the coast is clear. May I suggest, Madame Wang Li, that you call Cha Li, and tell her and her companions to remain where they are until I arrive there."

Madame Wang Li made the call immediately, and everyone present was pleased to hear that the girls were safe – for the time being at least.

"Then I'd better be on my way," said Inspector Chan. "The sooner I can talk to them in person, the better."

"Would it be possible for me to accompany you inspector?" asked Henry. "There are a few other things I would like to discuss with you, and we could talk during the car journey."

"Of course you can," replied the inspector. "It will give us a chance to become better acquainted. If you will excuse us, ladies, we'll be on our way." He bowed low, in the customary Chinese way, before shaking hands with Mary and Madame Wang Li.

"Be assured that the girls will soon be back in the safe residence, and this unpleasant episode will be behind you."

Chapter 13

Merlin's Warning

Following the gathering in the royal tent, King Arthur and his aides visited the field hospital where the wounded and dying lay. Merlin escorted the boys to their sleeping quarters, and left them in the care of the knights assigned by the king to ensure their safety. He then retired to his own tent where his valet had prepared his supper. He sat in front of a log fire and, as he ate, he stared into the leaping flames.

"Are you all right, sire?" asked the valet with some concern as Merlin appeared to drift away into some kind of trance.

"I'm fine, thank you Dafydd, just tired. I'll be fine in the morning. You go to bed now, and don't worry about me any more tonight."

Dafydd knew that it was the time to retire, for he had witnessed this scene many times before as Merlin fell into a deep trance from which he could not be roused. He knew that Merlin travelled into another world through space and time while in these trances, of which Dafydd had no knowledge. They were mysterious places where Merlin had visions and this is why people regarded him as a magician with far-seeing powers.

As he looked deep into the flames Merlin's eyelids began to flicker, quickly at first, but then gradually more slowly, and each time his eyes opened he saw images in the leaping flames which transported him to a particular place. One place had four large rivers flowing eastwards, and from the four rivers leapt four dragons. He knew immediately that these were very special dragons because they were water dragons, each one living in one of the four great rivers of China. He knew this because he had seen them before many centuries before when Draco, the great dragon spirit, had spoken to him and told him that the Chinese Emperor Qin and his kingdom were in grave danger from attacking warlords from the north. This had been the first time that Draco had given Merlin a set of dragons' teeth which would enable him to travel through time. To help the emperor he had had to travel back in time to 220 BC and it was the water dragons and the emperor's army who had proved victorious. With the help of the dragons, Merlin had worked his magic to whip up a ferocious cyclone from the China Sea which had brought hurricane-force winds and torrential rain to northern China. The storm had thrown the invading armies into disarray, and the Qin dynasty had survived.

Merlin relived these events while in his trance, but he also had a vision of what was to come in the future. What he saw alerted him to the dangers which Huw, Arthur and his friends would face in the near future and he had to warn them as soon as he awoke.

He felt a hand on his shoulder trying to wake him. "Sire, it's time for your breakfast now," said Dafydd.

"What, already?" replied Merlin. "But I've only just fallen asleep haven't I?"

"No, sire," Dafydd smiled. "You must have fallen asleep in front of the log fire. I came to see if you were all right and wrapped you in a warm blanket where you lay. But that was ten hours ago!"

"What?" cried Merlin. "But there's something urgent I need to see to, something that can't wait. I need to see the boys!"

"All right," said Dafydd. "If you promise me you'll eat your breakfast, I'll go and fetch the boys right away."

"Would you do that for me Dafydd, that would be a great help, and yes I promise I'll eat some breakfast."

Dafydd grinned broadly, and left the tent immediately to search for the boys. He knew his master well, and that he had received a vision during the night and he had to find the boys without delay.

Huw and Arthur had just finished breakfast when Dafydd called them from outside their tent.

"I'm sorry to disturb you boys, but Merlin has instructed me to bring you to his tent immediately. He says it is a matter of some urgency!"

"Who are you?" asked Arthur through the tent opening.

"My name is Dafydd, and I am Merlin's valet and personal guard."

Arthur stepped outside and, seeing Merlin's crest on Dafydd's tunic, he shook his hand and called out to Huw to join them. A few minutes later they were all seated in Merlin's tent, and he began to tell them of the vision he saw during the night.

"I saw both of you in Xi'an province in northern China searching for the treasures of Emperor Qin but this was some time in the future because the emperor died in 210 BC. He was buried in a large tomb with most of his treasures, and also weapons to protect himself in the next world."

Huw and Arthur looked at Merlin in disbelief.

"But we know nothing of China," said Huw, "and why would we be searching for the emperor's tomb?"

Arthur recalled Mike's phone call. "There was something I meant to tell you Huw, but it slipped my mind with everything else going on. Your dad called me at the stables when I was there searching for you, after you'd first gone missing. He said that Mary and Henry had received an invitation to take Ivory to China so she could take part in the Hong Kong Challenge Gold Cup along with Ebony, and that we were all invited to go too."

"There," said Merlin, "so you will be going to China just as I saw in my vision."

"But even if we do go there," said Huw, "why would we be interested in the emperor's treasures. I just don't understand?"

"I'm not completely sure myself," said Merlin, "but I did notice that you were being followed when you were there, and judging by the appearance of the men I saw, I would guess that you were in immediate danger. That's why I called you here urgently this morning, to forewarn you of what might lie ahead."

"Do you think the men you saw in your vision might be there to steal the emperor's treasure?" asked Huw searching for some explanation.

"That's a distinct possibility," replied Merlin, "because he was an extremely rich man. However, they wouldn't know exactly where to find the treasure. You may, at some point in the future, have information that they don't, and that's why they are following you."

"Can you suggest a way that might help us to outwit them when the time comes?" asked Arthur.

"I think I can," replied Merlin, "but it won't be easy, and it will involve you in more time travel!"

Huw and Arthur looked at one another uneasily, for they knew the dangers involved in time travel and they already felt a long way from home.

"What would we have to do?" asked Arthur.

"I suggest you go and talk to Emperor Qin!"

"What?" exclaimed Arthur, "but that would mean having to go

back to around 212 BC wouldn't it, and how can we be sure that we would be safe doing that? After all, we haven't got your special powers have we?"

"Ah," replied Merlin confidently, "you see young man I have something here that was given to me by Emperor Qin, and whoever is in possession of this figure will be guaranteed safe passage in ancient China."

"So what exactly is it?" asked Huw.

"Here, see for yourself," said Merlin holding it out and placing it in Huw's hand. "It's a small figure of Buddha carved in jade. It's very precious, and has extraordinary powers. There are only two in existence and the emperor only gave one to me as he knew he could trust me implicitly."

As Huw took hold of the jade figure he felt his hand tingling, as if he had pins and needles, and then a powerful force spread through his arm and gradually engulfed his whole body. Arthur looked at Huw in astonishment. His eyes had turned green.

Chapter 14

Chan contacts Mabon

After talking to Mr Padfield, the boys' history teacher, DCI Mabon returned to police headquarters to see if any new information had arrived there. The receptionist told him that a call had come through from M16 asking the chief inspector to contact them immediately.

Mabon wasted no time making the call, and was soon speaking with a senior intelligence officer. The officer informed Mabon that Interpol had notified them of two sinister developments in China. Firstly, evidence was being gathered by Chinese intelligence that a terrorist plot was being planned, but so far the evidence was flimsy. Secondly, they had received a telephone call from an Inspector Chan in Hong Kong expressing concern about three girls staying in a safe residence, and how they had been followed by a group of men until they found refuge in Cha Li's friend's house. Apparently one of the girls was known to Inspector Mabon.

Mabon acted quickly on the message he had just received and within minutes was speaking to DCI Chan.

"Hello," said Mabon. "I understand that a girl from my home district may be in serious danger in Hong Kong. Is that true?"

"Yes," replied Chan, "I'm afraid so."

"Who is the girl?"

"Her name is Samantha Grant."

"Oh, yes indeed, I know Sam, as her friends call her, and her parents Mary and Henry Grant. Could you tell me exactly what's happened?"

"Well, she and her two friends, who are staying in a so-called safe residence here in Hong Kong, decided to visit the Ten Thousand Buddhas Monastery which was not far from their residence. Not sensing any danger Samantha's parents gave permission for the visit. After entering the monastery the girls visited a Chinese tearoom nearby for some refreshments. While there, they observed a group of men behaving suspiciously and after they left they noticed that they were being followed by some of the men. Fortunately, one of the girls – a local girl named Cha Li, took refuge in her best friend's house where they are now temporarily safe."

"Thank goodness for that," said Mabon breathing a sigh of relief. "If there's any way I can help you, then please let me know."

"Well, as a matter of fact, there is," said Chan speaking in perfect English. "Samantha's parents told me that you have first-hand experience in dealing with terrorist groups."

"That's true!"

"Well, we have been gathering evidence of a terrorist plot here in China and, as you know, Interpol is encouraging police forces worldwide to co-operate with one another and exchange information."

"Of course," said Mabon, "that would be the sensible thing to do, and yes we have encountered terrorist activity here in the last few years. In fact, we have a problem here right now because two of our local boys are missing, and so far we have no clear leads. The two boys are Huw and Arthur Pendry and are friends of Samantha."

"May I suggest," said Chan, "that we exchange information

regarding these separate incidents so that we can assist one another in our enquiries and investigations."

"Yes, of course," replied Mabon, "that's an excellent idea. I'll send you the information we have on file regarding terrorist activity here, and perhaps you could respond from there. May I suggest that we send information in coded form using Interpol's high security network."

"I couldn't agree more. I look forward to hearing from you, and good luck with your search for the boys."

"Good luck to you too, and please give my best wishes to Sam's parents. Maybe we shall meet in person soon," said Mabon not realizing quite how prophetic his words were...

*

After replacing the telephone, Mabon sat in his office thinking deeply about his conversation with Chan and his concerns about the whereabouts of Huw and Arthur. Could there be a connection between the missing boys and what was happening to Sam in Hong Kong? It didn't seem possible, but then he recalled the messages he had received from MI6 and Interpol. There was growing concern everywhere about the increase in global terrorism. He decided he must act quickly by first returning to the stables to see if Mike and the officers had any new leads on the boys' whereabouts. Then, he would probably have to consider travelling to Hong Kong as soon as possible to investigate Chan's concerns for the safety of the girls and growing evidence of global crime networks.

"Anything new?" asked Mabon on his return to the stables.

"Nothing yet," said Mike, "but we're all working hard to solve the problem, especially with the help of your officers. They've been absolutely great!"

"Good," said Mabon nodding to his men who were down on their knees sifting for anything that might be evidence and give them a lead.

"I've had some more bad news from Hong Kong too," said Mabon. "Sam and her girlfriends have been followed by some sinister-looking men, but luckily they were near Cha Li's friend's house and took refuge there. Thankfully the Chinese police are on the case."

"I'm sorry to hear that," said Mike. "Nothing seems to be working out right at the moment."

"Don't worry," said Mabon, "my instincts tell me that everything will be OK soon. The secret is to keep searching, and not to give up hope. I do have a problem, though."

"What's that?" asked Mike.

"I think I might have to leave for Hong Kong right away, but I'm not happy about leaving things unresolved here."

"You shouldn't be worrying about that," said Mike generously, "they obviously need you there where there could be more at stake. I'll carry on the search here, but if I could borrow your officers then that would be a big bonus."

"Of, course you can," said Mabon smiling. "I'll have a word with them now before I leave, but I know you can rely on them. Please let me know as soon as you have any news."

"I will," said Mike, "and thanks again. Oh, and by the way I shall be leaving for Hong Kong myself in two days' time. I have to make preparations for the Gold Cup. I'll look out for you when I get there."

"Excellent," replied Mabon, "and I shall leave DS Olwen Guest in charge of the investigation. She is a very capable officer who is respected by everyone in the squad."

"Thank you," said Mike, "and good luck in Hong Kong!"

Chapter 15

Mabon arrives in Hong Kong

Twenty-four hours after leaving Mike at the stables, DCI Mabon arrived at Hong Kong International airport. He was met on the tarmac by Chan in a Hong Kong Special Branch Police car driven by a young police officer named Tai.

Mabon joined Chan in the rear seats, and Chan explained that they had been given official clearance by airport security to bypass customs and excise. They were soon speeding along the North Lantau Expressway which connects the modern Hong Kong Airport to the city itself. Mabon marvelled at the construction of this highway which stretched from Lantau Island in the west, across the smaller islands of Ma Wan, Tsing Yi, and Ngong Shuen Chau, the stonecutters island where the rock was quarried for the highway. Long sweeping flyovers linked the islands together. To the north lay the open sea channel called Urmston Road as the expressway ran parallel to the coastline, whilst to the south the interior of Lantau Island rose to a height of 1,000 metres inside the richly forested Lantau Nature Reserve.

"We are heading north-east now," said Chan, bringing Mabon back down to earth with a jolt. He had been daydreaming since the police car left the airport, transfixed by the beauty of the land and seascapes around him. It was very different from those that he had left behind in the borderland of Wales.

"Are we going directly to Sha Tin and the safe residence?" asked Mabon.

"No," replied Chan, "I thought it best if we went straight to Cha Li's grandparents' house so that we can speak to the girls directly and get a clearer picture of exactly what happened when they visited the teahouse near the Ten Thousand Buddhas Monastery, and then how they managed to escape the men who followed them. A lot has happened since our last telephone call, but I'm really glad you were able to come so quickly."

"I was very lucky to get such an early flight," said Mabon, "but I was anxious to meet you and compare notes. But first things first, how did Cha Li and the other girls manage to shake-off their pursuers?"

"Good question," replied Chan, "but then Cha Li is a very bright girl, and she also knows the district around the monastery very well. They were able, thanks to her quick-thinking, to outwit the men in black through the narrow streets and winding alleyways. But they were a long way away from Cha Li's grandparents' house which is south of the Lion Rock Country Park." Chan pointed out the location of the park on a detailed map of Hong Kong which he passed to Mabon. Chan traced the route they were following with his finger so that Mabon could see where they were heading. He could also see where *they* were at that exact moment from the advanced Sat Nav system which was installed in the police car.

"So where exactly is Cha Li's grandparents' house?" asked Mabon.

"This will be a nice surprise for you!" exclaimed Chan pointing to a district immediately south of Lion Rock Park. "This is the area known as Beacon Hill, and the house is in Rhondda Road."

"Rhondda Road!" said Mabon with a broad grin on his face. "I don't believe it!" But there it was staring him straight in the eye. "That's a long way from the Ten Thousand Buddhas Monastery. They couldn't have walked that far surely?"

"No, my friend, they had to devise a plan to take them safely away from Cha Li's friend's house and south to the Beacon Hill district. It was an audacious plan, which thankfully worked out well, but it was not without mishap."

"Something went wrong? Was it serious?" asked Mabon looking worried.

"I think it would be best if Cha Li and the other girls explained what happened themselves. Take it easy inspector, we're almost there now. Then you'll know the answer to your questions," said Chan with a faint, tantalising smile which left Mabon feeling anxious.

Chapter 16

Emperor Qin

Merlin looked on as Huw and Arthur mounted XCalibur, adjusted the dragon's teeth to read 'City of Xi'an, China, 212 BC – The Emperor's Palace', and then bid the boys good luck as they once again entered the time portal. With a sudden whoosh they were back in the long dark tunnel travelling at the speed of light. Within moments they could see a blue light at the end of the tunnel, and then came the jolt as XCalibur touched down in what appeared to be a large courtyard surrounded by red coloured buildings with upward curling double-eaved roofs.

The moment they landed they were surrounded by palace guards who seemed to emerge from nowhere, each one holding a spear horizontally in a hostile manner. Huw pulled the jade Buddha from his pocket, and immediately the guards lowered their spears and knelt down as they recognised the emperor's talisman. Only the captain of the Royal Guard remained standing, and it was he who spoke first.

"As you bear the jade talisman of the emperor, then I bid you welcome to the Royal Palace of Xi'an. My name is Captain Zhong and it will be my privilege to escort you to the Emperor."

He held out his right hand to help the boys dismount. As he had been speaking Mandarin Chinese, they had no idea exactly what he had said, but as he was smiling at them they were no longer afraid. Captain Zhong gave an order to one of the guards to take XCalibur to the stables and watch him safely. No-one was to be allowed near him without the captain's express authority. Huw thanked the guard before removing his bag and whispering a few words in XCalibur's ear. The horse whinnied and nodded his head as if he understood, and then trotted off to the stable block at the far end of the courtyard.

Captain Zhong led the boys up a long flight of stone steps which were bordered by large statues of dragons painted in bright colours of blue, red and green. As they neared the top, huge wooden doors began to open as if by magic. Orders were being passed around the palace as if they were carried by ghosts. Everywhere seemed quiet as they crossed the outer hallway which was as large as a great cavern. Only the patter of their footsteps echoed in the silence. The inner doors opened and they were led into the inner sanctum, the emperor's throne room. Huw and Arthur gasped at the sight before them. A richly decorated carpet in red and gold stretched out before them and, at the far end, sat the Emperor Qin on his golden throne.

He beckoned them to come forward and to their surprise he stood up and walked towards them with a broad smile on his regal face. Huw realised immediately that the emperor had recognised the jade Buddha which he had given to Merlin many years ago.

"Welcome to the Imperial Palace my young friends," said the emperor in perfect English.

"But how…?" Huw began to ask.

"The jade figure has spoken to me about your arrival, and I know that you must be very brave young men to come here like this. I also know that you are friends of Merlin, otherwise he would not have entrusted you with the jade Buddha."

"Well, Merlin did say that the figure possessed magical powers, but it's almost as if you can read our minds," continued Huw, looking awestruck.

"Yes, in a way I can," said the emperor, "such is the power of the jade Buddha. However, the power only works if you have the identical twin."

"You mean there are two jade Buddhas exactly alike, your Highness?" asked Arthur.

"Yes, indeed young man, and they are the only two identical twin Buddhas in existence. No other figures of Buddha are exactly alike."

"You mean they're like carbon copies of one another?"

"Er, yes!" smiled the emperor. "That's a nice way of putting it. Carbon copy, yes, I must remember that."

"But I can't believe your English is so faultless, your Highness, if you'll allow me to say so," chipped in Huw.

"Well, I'll let you into a secret," said the emperor. "You see it wouldn't be proper for me to take the credit for this. I'm actually speaking to you in Mandarin, in my thoughts, and the jade Buddha is translating my thoughts into your language so that when I speak you can understand me perfectly."

"But I can read your lips too!" exclaimed Huw.

"Precisely so," said the Emperor with an even broader smile, "such is the magical power of the two jade Buddhas."

Then as Huw and Arthur stood there with their mouths open in disbelief, the emperor reached into the left-hand pocket of his robe and removed the identical twin figure of the one Huw was holding tightly in his grasp. He felt a strong tingling sensation in his hand and shooting up his arm.

"Wow," said Huw, "it's stronger than the vibration from my mobile phone."

"Excuse me, what is a mobile phone?" asked the emperor.

Arthur fell about laughing. He couldn't believe what he was hearing, and even the emperor's top General Meng Tian, who was standing behind him, burst out laughing!

"Come," said the emperor trying to keep a straight face, "enough of this frivolity, we must talk seriously about why you have come here to Xi'an. But first we must eat and drink."

He clapped his hands and everyone, including General Tian and Captain Zhong, bowed deeply and backed away while he led Huw and Arthur towards the entrance to the grand banqueting hall. Once inside, Emperor Qin led them to the furthest end of a very long table. It must have been at least 200 metres long, thought Huw as he counted the number of paces it took him before a footman ushered him to a plush chair upholstered in red and gold. The emperor sat at the end with a large window behind him which looked out on a beautiful garden. Huw and Arthur sat facing one another with General Meng Tian next to Huw and Captain Zhong alongside Arthur.

Emperor Qin clapped his hands and a myriad of servants appeared from nowhere. It seemed as if everything had been carefully planned in advance, even though the Emperor couldn't have known they were coming – could he? General Tian whispered to Huw that this was going to be a very special meal, only prepared for VIPs. Huw glanced at Arthur who was all ears and was wearing his trademark grin. Huw noticed a brief smile flitting across the emperor's face as he anticipated their reactions to the servants' movements. Each one had been trained to perfection and they moved around the table like silent ghosts.

A menu written in Mandarin and English was placed before them and Huw's eyes opened wide as he saw that the first course was to be shark's fin soup. When it arrived it smelled and looked delicious, and as Huw glanced up he saw the emperor place the palms of his hands together before saying a short prayer. Everyone followed suit until the emperor had finished. Then with a brief nod he smiled at each of his guests and invited them to begin.

It soon became obvious that this was not going to be a relaxing lunch, as the emperor asked Huw to outline the reason for their visit.

"Well, sir," began Huw, who decided to get straight to the point, "we have spoken to Merlin who advised us to speak to you directly. We have uncovered a plot to break into your sacred tomb. We know that this is planned to happen in the 21st century AD which is the time in which we live in. The thieves are planning to steal your most valuable possessions and treasures."

The emperor's eyes opened wide in surprise and horror at the prospect of his sacred burial place being invaded and plundered at some time in the distant future.

"But this would be desecration of the worst kind!" exclaimed General Tian angrily, spluttering through his shark's fin soup.

"I'm sorry to upset you like this," said Huw, "but Arthur and I thought it best to warn you of Merlin's prediction. I'm sure you know, sir, how accurately he can see the future in his visions."

"Yes, of course," replied the emperor, "please stay calm everyone." He glanced at General Tian and Captain Zhong as he spoke, and they bowed their heads towards the emperor as if asking for his forgiveness. "Everything will be all right," he continued, smiling gently, "if we begin making plans immediately. We are so fortunate to have received this warning from our young guests, and we must build on this knowledge."

As they sat pondering over the emperor's wise words the servants brought in the second course which was jellyfish and chicken salad. Arthur looked up at Huw in surprise as he tasted his first piece of jellyfish. It wasn't like jelly at all but had a delicious crunchy texture. They were never going to forget this meal.

"Your Highness," said Arthur, trying to maintain a straight face as he munched happily on a mouthful of jellyfish strips, "how can you be sure that everything will be all right in 2,000 years' time?"

"Well Arthur," replied the emperor with a knowing smile. He was so delighted to see the boys enjoying themselves that he seemed totally relaxed about the future. "We began preparations on the Imperial Tomb back in 221 BC when I was ordained as the first Imperial Emperor of all China, so a great deal has been achieved already. When we finish our meal then I will show you a model of the tomb which was designed by my chief architect, and I can assure you that nothing has been left to chance. But first let us enjoy dessert, I feel sure you will approve of that!"

As he finished speaking he clapped his hands and the silent servants glided in with the fabulous dessert. Huw and Arthur couldn't believe their eyes as they looked down on plates filled with small coconut tartlets with a golden brown topping of caramelised sugar and roasted peanuts. Alongside each plate was a bowl of lychee ice cream. They only knew this because a printed card was placed above each dish in Mandarin and English of course!

*

When the meal was over Huw and Arthur thanked the emperor sincerely for treating them to an unforgetable experience. What a feast it had been. But now it was time to think once again about

Merlin's warning. The emperor led them into his stateroom which was regarded as highly secret and only entered by his top military generals and court advisers. He showed them an open-topped model of the Imperial Tomb. Huw and Arthur gasped at the sheer scale of the model, and the range of preparations that were being made for the death of the emperor and his entry into the spirit world. The tomb itself was surrounded by dozens of sunken pits in which the boys could see that the architect had placed small toy soldiers dressed in uniforms of many colours and styles. There were rows and rows of them, probably thousands, certainly too many to count.

Huw looked quizically at General Tian who, with the emperor's permission, began to explain. "This represents the armed forces that will accompany the emperor into the spirit world and protect him from any harm which might befall him. They will be created from clay and bronze and will come to life if the emperor commands it through the power of the jade Buddha. You already know of its magical powers which have brought you here today. So nothing is being left to chance, we must think again."

As Huw looked at the model he was trying to remember the inside of the ancient burial mound Twmp Trellech where King Arthur and Culhwch had been buried. He recalled the spiral patterns of the passageways inside the mound and looked to see if there was anything like that in the model of the Imperial Tomb. But he could see nothing similar. He turned to General Tian and explained his thoughts on the spiral patterns. The general understood and turned to the emperor to explain.

"Thank you Huw," he said graciously. "You have given us much to think about. We must think again about ways to deceive and divert grave robbers who might invade the Imperial Tomb at some future time. We are greatly indebted to you for bringing this to our attention. Your concern for our safety and well-being is most admirable, and we will not forget you or your cousin Arthur."

Chapter 17

Huw's Dad
leaves for Hong Kong

Mike stood in XCalibur's stable staring at the wall which had
metamorphosed into blue glass. Was it possible that the boys could
have passed through a time portal in this wall? He reached out his
hand to touch it, but then stopped as he recalled the previous time
when his arm had disappeared up to the elbow and he had felt a
powerful force sucking him in.

He felt his mobile phone vibrating on his belt.

"Hello," he said hoping to hear Huw's voice, but it was his
brother Morgan – Arthur's father – calling from Pendry Farm.

"Hi Mike, is there any good news I can give to Rachel about
the boys? She's very tearful and asking me to call you every ten
minutes. I keep telling her that you'll call us if there's any change,
but she's so anxious."

"It's all right Mog, I understand how she feels, but there's still
no definite news yet. The police have called in DCI Mabon who has
a squad of special investigators on the case, and we're hoping for
some good news soon. Mabon is following some strong leads and is
convinced that he will get to the bottom of this mystery soon. Tell
Rachel to keep busy, and that everything possible is being done."

"Thanks Mike, I'll pass on your message to Rachel right away. She'll be pleased to hear that Mabon is involved."

Mog sounded slightly reassured, and Mike thought he'd better inform him now of his imminent departure for Hong Kong.

"I'm flying out to Hong Kong tomorrow Mog, as the time for the Hong Kong Challenge Gold Cup is drawing near. As you know, Mary and Henry Grant are already out there with Ivory as guests of Sheikh Rashid. I will be staying with them until the race meeting at Sha Tin is over, but I will be in regular contact with the investigating team here at the stables. Forensics are involved, so we can expect to get some answers soon. Don't worry about anything here; DCI Mabon and his second-in-command DS Olwen Guest will be constantly in touch with me and with Mary Grant who owns the stables."

"Good luck for the race meeting," said Mog, "and please give our best wishes to the Grant family!"

Chapter 18

Cha Li's Grandparents' House

They were seated around the long table in Cha Li's grandparents' dining room. Nanna Yin Li and Pappa Yang Li sat at the head of the table with the girls down the right-hand side and the DCIs Chan and Mabon opposite.

Once the introductions had been made DCI Chan came straight to the point. "DCI Mabon and I would like to know exactly what happened when you left Lin Tong's parents' house to escape from the men in black who were stalking you?"

"Well, that's where the incredible plan kicked in," answered Cha Li. "You see, Lin Tong texted some of our friends to come to her house after dark and bring their bikes with them."

"You mean you planned to come here on bikes?"

"Seemed like a good idea at the time, but after dark of course! We knew they were watching the house, but the back garden leads to a small woodland through which runs a narrow path. We all knew it well, and that's how we made our escape and then headed for the western edge of Lion Rock Country Park."

"You all knew this park well?"

"Oh yes, we often picnicked there in the summer, and

sometimes cycled right through to the southern edge of the park to visit my grandparents here in Rhondda Road." She smiled at her grandparents. "We always knew we would receive a warm welcome here and Nanna and Pappa always said 'the more the merrier'." Everyone laughed at this, especially Nanna and Pappa. "Some of Lin Tong's friends lent their bikes to Sam and Sheba and the group headed off at first light. We rode south, keeping close to the park's western edge where there is plenty of shrubbery and woodland cover. We skirted Lion Rock which is the highest point in the park."

Chan pointed this out to Mabon on the map, and he could see it was quite high at 495 metres.

"Then one of the girls had a puncture," continued Cha Li, "and as we dismounted our bikes a group of cyclists emerged from the early morning mist and rode straight up to us. We did feel frightened as the riders were all wearing black hooded cloaks."

"Oh no," said Mabon, "had the men in black caught up with you?"

"Thankfully no," said Cha Li. "You see they were novice nuns from the nearby Chi Lin Buddhist Nunnery taking their early morning exercises. They dismounted and came towards us, removing their hoods. Their leader, Sister Milefo, explained who they were and that, as part of her duties, she had to mentor the novice nuns. Some of their training meant that they had to become mobile so they could eventually work in the community. Bikes were their main form of transport."

"What sort of nuns were they?" asked Chan.

"They live at the Chi Lin Buddhist Nunnery on the eastern side of the park. We were frightened at first because they have shaven heads, and are not allowed to walk or ride in public without wearing cloaks and hoods. Sister Milefo could see we needed help with the puncture, but she soon realised something more serious was wrong. So I quickly explained our predicament and that there was every possibility that the men in black – the cobramen – might pick up their tracks and come after us again."

"Did she understand just how dangerous these men were?" asked Mabon.

"Oh yes, she was very perceptive and streetwise, and reassured us that the men in black would not dare to approach them as it is forbidden in China for either nuns or monks to be molested or hurt in any way. They were protected by the divine laws of Buddha, and even hardened criminals were afraid to breach those laws. She then supervised the novice nuns who helped fixed the puncture, and afterwards gave us some spare cloaks she was carrying in her cycle trolley. Soon we were all dressed as novice nuns, and she insisted on escorting us all to the Wong Tai Sin Temple at the southern end of the park – apparently the temple is a very busy place and she would help us take refuge there during the day and then help to smuggle us out the following night and bring us here safely, and here we are!" Cha Li was beaming now at DCIs Chan and Mabon.

"What a story!" exclaimed DCI Mabon, "and we're all so glad you arrived here safely." He glanced at DCI Chan and said, "now we have to make sure you stay safe!"

"That won't be easy," said Pappa Yang Li. "You see, chief inspector, these are all adventurous girls and they won't be able to sit still for long if they're all like Cha Li."

Everyone laughed out loud whilst Nanna Yin Li slipped out into the kitchen to provide something nice for tea. She had already prepared many Dim sum dishes, which are offered to guests in a buffet-style meal so that everyone could choose their favourites. Cha Li followed her into the kitchen to help, and soon they were carrying the dishes into the dining room and placing them on a side table. There were delectable dumplings – or pot-stickers as they are known – of chicken, prawn, pork and shrimp. There were Shanghai spring rolls containing mushrooms, cabbage and sprouts, all accompanied by traditional dips, scallops and Chinese radish balls, fish wrapped in Tofu skin, shrimp toast, and for dessert sweet filled wantons (golden surprise, stuffed bananas, caramelised pineapple, vanilla, honey and saffron pears and toffee apples).

Everyone was in high spiirits, and what a tea party it was going to be. As they all chatted away over the table, Cha Li whispered quietly to Mabon that she would show him the coded messages as soon as the festivities were over.

Chapter 19

Departures and Arrivals

Huw and Arthur felt quite sad when the time came to say their farewells to Emperor Qin and his staff at the Imperial Palace. They crossed the courtyard to the large stable block where XCalibur had been fed and watered and looked after by the emperor's grooms throughout the night. His eyes were bright and his coat was shining like never before.

"Wow," said Huw as he patted him gently on his shoulder, "you look magnificent. If you were a little bit older we could enter you for the Hong Kong Challenge Gold Cup in a few days' time."

"You must be patient," replied the emperor, "he is still a young colt. But from his bearing I would say he will be a champion one day and you will be very proud of him. Now you must prepare to leave, but what is your next destination?"

"Well, I had a vivid dream last night."

"And were you by any chance holding the jade Buddha when you went to sleep?"

"Yes, I was," said Huw, "but how did you know?"

"Well, I often do it myself," replied the emperor, "because it brings me great comfort and also helps me see into the future."

"That's exactly what happened last night, and in my dream I saw my father arriving in Hong Kong Airport."

"Airport! What is airport?"

"It's where aeroplanes take off and land," chipped in Arthur, feeling a bit left out of the conversation.

"Do you mean flying objects?" asked General Meng Tian. "I have been reading about some of our inventors carrying out experiments which will help them to fly like a large black-necked crane."

"That's right," said Arthur, "but these aircraft can carry hundreds of people from one part of the world to the other."

"I must look into this matter more seriously," said the emperor, "it sounds promising. But first we must focus on your dream, and you must find your father without delay, Huw. Something tells me that it is vitally important you meet with him soon, so you must follow your dream and travel without delay to Hong Kong. Do not waste time by returning home. I think there is much more at stake than the Hong Kong Challenge Gold Cup which you mentioned!"

"But how do I know that what I saw in my dream is true?" asked Huw.

"The jade Buddha is never wrong. You have been given an insight into what is to come, and your father is beckoning you to follow him to Hong Kong."

"Are you very sure about this, your Highness? I greatly respect your wisdom but..."

"Have no doubts, young Huw. You see I also had a dream – perhaps the same one as yourself because I too was holding my jade Buddha when I said my prayers last night. I prayed to Buddha that you, Arthur and XCalibur would be returned safely to your family today. I also saw your father arriving in Hong Kong and he told an official that he needed to be transported to somewhere called the 'safe residence'. You must now make haste and join him there."

Huw and Arthur bowed to the emperor, shook hands with General Meng Tian and Captain Zhong. They also thanked the grooms for taking such good care of XCalibur. Everyone watched in wonder as Huw and Arthur manipulated the dragon's teeth to read 'The Safe Residence, Hong Kong, December 2012'. They placed the leather cord around the horse's neck, and then mounted.

"I won't forget what you said about the spiral patterns and I shall attend to it immediately. I wish you a safe journey and that Buddha will guard you against evil forces when you return to the future."

The emperor waved his final farewell, and his military officers saluted.

The ground rumbled and soon Huw, Arthur and XCalibur found themselves in the long dark tunnel travelling through time and space faster than the speed of light.

*

Mike fastened his seatbelt as the giant Airbus passenger jet aircraft prepared for its descent into Hong Kong International Airport on Lantau Island. It had been a long tiring journey since departure at Heathrow Airport, but now he was almost there and really looking forward to seeing Mary and Henry Grant, his close friends and employers. He could also picture Sam, Mary's daughter, helping him with grooming duties at the stables on Grant Court Estate where he was head trainer. Sam loved Ivory very much and, though she was still at school, she spent most of her free time looking after the champion mare, and her two-year-old colt, XCalibur. Although Mary had made a gift of XCalibur to Sheikh Rashid when the foal had been born, the sheikh had generously insisted that he should spend his early years growing up with his mother and his young stablemates.

He wasn't looking forward to explaining to Sam, and the others, that there was still no sign of Huw, Arthur, and XCalibur, and things were looking bleak. A tear fell from the corner of his eye at the horrible prospect of never seeing them ever again. His thoughts turned back to Pendry Farm where he and his brother Morgan had grown up as young boys. The farm was situated in the green hills of the Welsh borderlands, the Marches, and had belonged to his father Joseph Pendry, and before that to his grandfather Jacob Pendry, who was the eldest of six brothers – Morgan, Matthew, Samuel, Timothy and Joshua. His great-grandparents Paul Pendry and Molwen (Molly) had owned the farm way back in the 1800s and had been very religious, hence the Biblical names handed down through the generations. He was deep in nostalgic thoughts when the captain's voice interrupted via the intercom.

"This is the captain speaking. Please make sure that your seat belts are securely fastened as we are about to pass through some turbulent weather on our descent to the airport. If you look out through your windows you will see the storm clouds building up below us."

Mike looked out at the towering cumulonimbus clouds visibly growing below them. They were dark and purple-grey in colour and looked very threatening.

"Please remain calm," said the captain. "There will be some buffeting over the next ten minutes or so until we emerge beneath the cloud bank. Then you will all be able to relax when you see the runway approaching. We have received news from air traffic control that minor earth tremors have been reported across various parts of China but they have not resulted in any loss of life or serious damage to buildings. These tremors may have caused atmospheric disturbances leading to air turbulence. We are confident that our aircraft has been strongly built to deal with such weather conditions. I will speak to you again in approximately ten minutes from now, when all will be well."

The captain's voice broke off and some slight buffeting occurred as they descended into the cloud bank. Mike had this strange sensation that he was riding his childhood pony, Owain, through a long dark tunnel, and they were galloping into the face of a howling gale. The air was being forced through the tunnel with incredible force, and they had difficulty moving forward. Images of Huw and Arthur flickered before his eyes, and he imagined they were travelling through the tunnel with him. The vision suddenly passed and, as he looked through the aircraft window, the cloud was clearing and they were descending calmly towards the runway.

"There, that wasn't too bad after all was it!" exclaimed the captain. "I can now see the runway ahead and we shall soon be landing at Lantau. I wish you all a safe and happy stay in the wonderful city of Hong Kong!"

Mike sighed with relief that all was well, and he wondered if anyone would be there to meet him at the airport. He would soon find out!

Chapter 20

Cha Li talks to the two DCIs

Back at Cha Li's grandparents' house in Rhondda Road, everyone offered to lend a hand in the kitchen as there was a large amount of washing-up to be done. Everyone except Detective Chief Inspectors Chan and Mabon who went into the lounge to talk to Cha Li.

"Could you now show us the papers which you picked up in the teahouse?" asked Chan.

"Of course," replied Cha Li, "I have kept them safely locked up in Nanna Li's china cabinet so that they couldn't possibly get lost or stolen."

"Good thinking," said Chan as Cha Li unlocked the cabinet and produced the three sheets of paper which had been stapled together in the top left-hand corner.

Having removed the staple, Chan and Mabon spread them out on the coffee table. There were three coded messages, one for each page, which at first glance were completely indecipherable.

"This is not going to be easy," said Mabon who had gained plenty of experience in cracking codes when working with the Severnside Special Police Force. "Obviously the men in black, with images of cobras tattooed on their hands and arms, were determined to keep their plans secret for as long as possible so that there would be little chance of them being detected. The cobramen are certainly a streetwise criminal organisation who will stop at nothing to achieve their objectives."

"They certainly looked very sinister in the teahouse," said Cha Li, "and although I did my best to avoid their glances they must have become very suspicious of our presence there. But the truth was that we had only entered the teahouse for some light refreshments after visiting the Ten Thousand Buddhas Monastery. We only became aware of their presence because of the way they were dressed, and the fact that they whispered secretively to one another. They weren't chatting away happily as any normal group would be in the pleasant surroundings of the teahouse."

"You did very well to outsmart them when you left the teahouse," said Chan. "These guys obviously became aware of your presence but they were clever at concealing their thoughts. I'm surprised they were meeting in the teahouse in the first place; it's not exactly a good hiding place for a meeting is it? But that's the sort of mistake they sometimes make which gives us a chance to see into their dark world. I've not yet come across the perfect criminal. Each one leaves a clue, or clues, somewhere along their path, and that's how we are able to catch up with them eventually."

"Oh, I do hope you can stop them before they hit their targets, whatever those are," said Cha Li.

"Well, my first reaction to seeing these coded messages is that we'll need to get our heads together as soon as possible and see if we can crack the codes."

"My advice," said Chan "would be for you to leave your grandparents' house, so that they won't be put in danger."

"I agree," said Mabon "and I also understand that Mike is due to land at Hong Kong Airport very soon. So we will need to send transport there to pick him up. May I suggest Chan that we all transfer to the safe residence as Sheikh Rashid will have plenty of security in place there."

"I'll arrange transport for Mike right now," said Chan as he picked up his high security police mobile phone. "Then we all head for Fantastic Light where the serious work will commence. Would you go to the kitchen please Cha Li and inform the others of our plans? While you are doing that, I'll send for extra vehicles to transport us there as quickly as possible."

Cha Li nodded and headed straight off to tell the others. There was no time to lose; they had to move fast to outwit the cobramen.

"I hope Mike will bring some good news about the boys," said Mabon holding the coded messages tightly in his hand as he listened to DCI Chan talking to a member of his special forces team at Hong Kong Police headquarters.

Chapter 21

Cracking the Codes

No-one could possibly have anticipated what happened the moment they returned from Cha Li's grandparents' house to the safe residence, Fantastic Light. The residence lived up to its name. The front courtyard was lit up by rays of light coming from all directions. At first everyone was dazzled by the mixture of blue, white and yellow light. Everything that was real shimmered in the kaleidoscope of shapes and images. It seemed to Cha Li as if the spaceship she had seen in the film *E.T. the Extra-Terrestrial* was about to touch down.

Suddenly everyone was there: Mike alighted from his taxi bathed in a soft yellow light. Then Huw, Arthur and XCalibur appeared surrounded by an aura of blue light. Cha Li and Sam, with their friends and DCIs Chan and Mabon, were swathed in white light as they emerged from their police escort vehicles.

Mike dropped his travel bags and rushed across to embrace Huw and Arthur. He could hardly believe his eyes, but as he hugged Huw he knew he wasn't dreaming. "But what happened?" he asked in disbelief, "we've been searching for you for days... and how on earth did you arrive here?"

Everyone gathered around Huw and Arthur, and Sam threw her arms around XCalibur's neck in excitement. He shook his head and snorted, which was his way of saying hello!

Chan decided to take over and shouted orders for the stable hands to look after XCalibur while he led the others into the house. "We've obviously got a lot of catching up to do and there's a lot going on we don't understand. I suggest you all retire to your rooms for an hour and then perhaps we can all meet in the library. DCI Mabon and I will go there directly and start looking at the coded messages. We'll have to work out a plan to decode them as quickly as possible."

*

An hour later everyone had assembled in the library along with Madame Wang Li and Sheikh Rashid. Madame Wang Li had arranged some light refreshments and the mood was generally more relaxed than it was earlier in the courtyard.

Sheikh Rashid welcomed everyone to his residence and assured them they would all be safe while they were there.

"I have a high level of security in place here, so I can guarantee there should be no further problems regarding your personal safety and that of the horses. There are double the number of guards around the stables and the entire perimeter of the estate. We have two major concerns at the moment, firstly the preparations for the race meeting which takes place in three days' time on 17 December at Sha Tin Racecourse. Secondly, the threat posed by the organisation calling themselves cobramen. I have already spoken to DCIs Chan and Mabon, and we are all agreed that the codes must be broken without delay. We suggest dividing into three groups – let's call them A, B and C. I will join Mary, Henry and Mike in Group A; DCI Chan will join Cha Li, Sam and Sheba in Group B and DCI Mabon will join

Huw, Arthur and Ahmed in Group C. We must begin immediately and use our wits to crack these codes and stop these evil men before it is too late."

Everyone nodded in agreement, and the three groups assembled at different points of the large room. Sheikh Rashid led Mary, Henry and Mike to his favourite part of the library which contained hundreds of books on the breeding and training of thoroughbreds. Between the bookcases were photographs, paintings and sketches of horses from the Sheikh's stables which had won many trophies around the world. These included the Epsom Derby, the Dubai World Cup, the Kentucky Derby and the Hong Kong Challenge Gold Cup.

Mary was holding the coded message which their group had been given, and as they gathered around a small table she placed it in the middle where they could all see clearly and then she turned it around and looked at it from different angles. A draft from an open window caught the sheet and turned it over. As Mary reached out to correct it, Henry called out.

"Wait a moment, there are faint markings on the back of the sheet, and... yes I can just make out one or two words."

He picked up the sheet and walked to a mirror which hung between two of the bookcases.

"That's it," he cried, "I've got it!"

Everyone crowded around to see the image Henry was looking at:

Sha Tin Racecourse – Hong Kong Challenge Gold Cup – Hack into Computer System

The first coded message had been cracked!

"But how were you so quick to see that?" asked Sheikh Rashid.

"Probably due to my pilot's training," replied Henry. "You see we are trained to look at images from all angles, including upside down. But also we have to be quick to make sense of messages which have been scrambled. What we are looking at here is a mirror image of the actual message. As the draft from the window turned the page over, the bright light enabled me to see the words through the paper."

"Well done Henry," said Sheikh Rashid, "but I'm afraid the news is not good. Look at the rest of the message everyone."

Everyone remained silent as they read through the message:

Transfer all bets... Remove three Buddhas from monastery... Remove handcrafted costumes used in Cantonese Opera

"What shall we do first?" asked Mary.

"I will alert all my security guards immediately," replied Sheikh Rashid, "and inform DCIs Chan and Mabon so that special police forces can be dispatched to the monastery."

"Computer surveillance will have to be heightened too," added Mike. "They may have already hacked into the system to divert funds into their own bank accounts."

*

DCI Chan, Cha Li, Sam and Sheba, who together formed Group B were huddled together in a small alcove in the library. The second coded message was baffling everyone and they each had a notebook in which they were scribbling away frantically when suddenly Cha Li said, "Got it!"

"Have you cracked it?" asked Sam.

"Think so!"

"Well, let us in on the secret formula then."

"I noticed that the second word in the message began and ended with the same letter – L," said Cha Li. "So I substituted other letters for the two Ls until I came up with two Ms. What they've done is taken the preceding letter from the alphabet and substituted it for the actual letter. So in the coded message L is actually M. I then applied this to the other letters until LTRDTL became MUSEUM."

"Well done Cha Li," said DCI Chan. "Let's see what we can make of it."

Before long the second message became clearer, and the inspector was looking deeply concerned. He began to read the decoded message out slowly:

Shanghai History Museum... Remove several jias [wine vessels]; also best pieces of Three Coloured Ceramics and Celadon Ware... Remove two large jade Buddhas from Jing'an Temple.

"We must confer with the other two groups and work out a plan of action without delay."

*

DCI Mabon met with Huw, Arthur and Ahmed in the reference room adjoining the main library. The third coded message looked a jumble of dots and dashes, but it was that which gave Mabon the first clue.

"I've seen something like this before looking through old Second World War messages. It reminds me of Morse code."

"What's Morse code?" asked Huw.

"Well, it's a method of sending messages by radio signals whereby short wave and long wave sounds transmitted in a certain order can be deciphered into letters and words. Each group of dots and dashes will give us a letter in the alphabet, so see if you can work out which letter is represented by three dashes, and which letter by three dots. Once we've worked out each letter, we can decode the message."

After ten minutes of hard work and cross referencing with each other they had worked out which symbol equalled which letter. Then they built up the sentences in the message.

"This is not good news," said Mabon gravely.

"This target is in Xi'an which is in north-central China. The cobramen are active in all parts of the country. This operation will not be easy to co-ordinate. Without going into great detail at this point, it is clear that they are targeting the Emperor Qin's burial chamber near Xi'an, and they are planning to enter the tomb and remove priceless treasures from there."

Huw glanced at Arthur knowingly and remembered Merlin's warning, and the meeting with Emperor Qin.

"I think we can help you with this part of your operation, inspector," said Huw. "You see, sir, Arthur and I have already been there!"

Chapter 22

Plan of Action

Saturday, 15 December 2012, was a day none of them would ever forget. When the children assembled for breakfast that morning they discovered that Sheikh Rashid and DCIs Chan and Mabon had drawn up detailed plans late last night for each of the three groups.

It was Sheikh Rashid who once again took the lead as they all sat down to eat their cereals. "I'm sorry this has to be a working breakfast," he said with a faint smile playing briefly on his lips, "but the next 24 hours are going to be critical. As you will see I've given each of you a typewritten schedule for your group. Group A, which includes myself, Mary, Henry and Mike will proceed to the Sha Tin Racecourse where there will be a full day's race meeting culminating in the Hong Kong Challenge Gold Cup at 4 p.m. Under normal circumstances this is always a very busy day at Sha Tin with 60,000 racegoers converging on the racecourse, together with horses, trainers, owners and jockeys from all over the world. Security is normally high, but today it will have to be doubled. DCI Chan has already alerted the Hong Kong Special Police Force, and DCI Mabon is in touch with Interpol. We are going to need all the help we can get to outsmart the cobramen and prevent a major disaster breaking out.

"Excuse me interrupting, your Highness," said Sam, "but I see from my schedule that Group B will be leaving Hong Kong at noon and that we shall be travelling by seaplane. Is that so?"

"Absolutely right Sam, you and your group will be led by DCI Chan and you will be travelling on a large police seaplane which is used by Hong Kong Special Police Forces at times of high security risk, such as right now!"

"And Group C, your Highness?" asked Huw. "How will we be travelling to Xi'an?"

Another smile from Sheikh Rashid. "You've got a great surprise in store, too! You're going to be flying to Xi'an on my private jet, along with DCI Mabon, and yes XCalibur will be able to fly too. I understand it's important that he goes with you!"

"Yes, your Highness, Merlin advised us that it was essential to the success of our mission."

"Very well then, so shall it be! Now, I suggest we relax a little and finish our breakfast, and then each of you can join your group and sort out the finer details. We will endeavour to remain in touch throughout the next few days and react accordingly to the information received. Good luck to you all, and now let's finish breakfast!"

By noon each of the three groups had left the safe residence. Sheikh Rashid led a convoy of trucks and horseboxes to Sha Tin Racecourse; DCI Chan led his group to Hong Kong harbour; and DCI Mabon's group left for the sheikh's private airstrip.

Chapter 23

The Hong Kong Challenge Gold Cup

As Sheikh Rashid's convoy made its way to the Sha Tin Racecourse just after noon, the crowds were already converging on the race meeting in their thousands. The police presence was high, as the sheikh had predicted, and additional security staff had been brought in. The Hong Kong Challenge Gold Cup was one of the largest and richest races in the international calendar for thoroughbred horse racing. To horse owners, the prestige of winning would bring huge rewards. Apart from the prize money itself, which carried a top prize of $25 million, there would be worldwide publicity, and huge fees could be charged if the winning horse went to stud.

Once they arrived at the racecourse they went straight to the special stables which they had been allocated. No members of the public were allowed to enter the stables zone, which was ring-fenced and monitored by security guards and cameras. As they began to prepare Ebony and Ivory for the big race later in the afternoon, news came in from the Special Police Force computer centre that serious disruption to the race betting and banking services – due to computer hacking – was being experienced.

"This must be due to interference by the cobramen," said Henry, who had been given special receiving equipment by DCI Chan to monitor what was going on. They all had to remain on high alert.

"Not much doubt about that," replied Mike. "Is anything else being reported?"

"Yes, and it confirms what we learned from the coded messages."

"Oh no, have any treasures been reported missing?"

"I'm afraid so," said Henry looking alarmed. "The cobramen have already broken into the Ten Thousand Buddhas Monastery and also the Heritage Museum, as predicted in the coded messages."

"But I thought security had already been tightened!"

"It has, but apparently some of the gang had entered the building during the day by hiding themselves among groups of tourists. Then they hid themselves away and came out after dark to steal the treasures. They overpowered the nightwatchman and smuggled the pieces out disguised as maintenance staff."

"Sounds like the operation was well planned; we're not dealing with amateur crooks," said Mike.

When Sheikh Rashid arrived on the scene Henry told him quickly of the reports coming in.

"They are acting on several fronts at the same time in order to distract and divert police force attention from the racecourse," replied the sheikh. "We must all be on our guard and keep a close eye on the horses at all times. Who knows what they might be capable of."

"Henry, Mary and I have already decided not to leave the horses unattended for one moment," said Mike, looking deadly serious.

"Thank you," says Sheikh Rashid, "I'm so glad you are all here today, it gives me more confidence, and I have doubled the number of security guards around the perimeter of the stables. I am taking no chances!"

A senior race steward arrived to inform them that they were expected to take their horses to the parade ring in 15 minutes when the time would be 3.30 p.m. The afternoon seemed to have flown by and now they made their final preparations to show the horses to the punters and other racegoers before the start of the big race.

As Mike led Ivory towards the parade ring he was followed by the sheikh's head trainer and top stable lad accompanying Ebony. Both horses looked magnificent and there were loud gasps and applause as the horses were led around the parade ring. Sheikh Rashid and Mary Grant, the owners, looked on proudly, while Henry was scanning the crowd with his binoculars to see if there were any suspicious-looking characters lurking behind the fence. It didn't take him long to spot someone. There was a man wearing dark sunglasses leaning against the racetrack railings on the other side of the course. He wasn't dressed in black, but Henry's sharp eyesight picked out a cobra tattoo on the man's hand. Before he could raise the alarm, a fanfare burst out with drums rolling, marching bands, bagpipes, fireworks and dancing dragons. A group of 100 athletes began a kung fu demonstration. The whole racecourse suddenly burst into life. It was mayhem. Henry lost sight of the man with the tattoo, and muttered angrily under his breath. He ran back towards the parade ring where the horses were beginning to make their way towards the starting line. Sheikh Rashid, Mike and Mary had now made their way to the VIPs box in the central stand, and Ebony and Ivory were left in the capable hands of their stable lads and jockeys who had now mounted the horses and were ready to canter back to the starting line. Henry made his way to the stand and prepared to alert the police and security guards.

Sheikh Rashid, Mary and Mike trained their binoculars on the starting line-up. Among the runners were Laaransaak, Montasur, Ninjago (a grey), Pawprints (with unusual markings looking like paws), Toga-Tiger, Daffydowndilly (a chestnut) and Arctic Lynx. Ebony and Ivory were in the middle of the pack as they lined up at the starting gates. Ebony was ridden by champion jockey Frankie Dettori who was one of Sheikh Rashid's favourite riders and who had already won the Hong Kong Challenge Gold Cup twice before. Ivory was being ridden by Willie Carson Jnr, who was riding in the Gold Cup for the first time.

Henry was busy talking to special forces police and other security staff when the starter's gun fired. The gates opened and the horses leapt forward. This was going to be some race – all 2,000 metres of it. Pawprints was the early leader, with the grey Ninjago just behind. Then came the main group of horses with one or two trailing behind as they rounded the first bend of the oval-shaped course. There were large TV screens placed around the course so that the 60,000 spectators could see in close-up exactly what was happening on the track. As they moved into the first straight a man suddenly jumped out in front of the horses. The two front runners, Pawprints and Ninjago, fell and the man was crushed beneath them. The other horses managed to avoid the fallers and the race continued. Police and paramedics were on the scene quickly, but it was soon clear that the man was dead. Luckily, neither the horses nor jockeys were seriously injured.

The race continued and, as they rounded the final bend, a group of four was pulling away from the others: Toga-Tiger was in the lead followed by Daffydowndilly. Ebony and Ivory were close on their heels. With two furlongs to go, Ebony and Ivory came up on the outside and swept past the leaders. At one furlong they were galloping head-to-head and neither of the jockeys was using a whip. As they crossed the line it was impossible to choose between them, and the stewards called a photo finish. The crowd held its breath, and a great silence settled over the racecourse. Then the result was announced over the speakers – it was a draw! Everyone went wild with excitement, as this was the first time ever that there been a draw in the Hong Kong Challenge Gold Cup.

Whilst everyone's eyes were now on the winners' enclosure where the two horses were led by their proud owners and trainers to where the presentations would be made, Henry made a beeline to where the paramedics were asking the special police officers for permission to remove the dead man's body to the local hospital.

"Has anything been found on the body?" asked Henry.

"Only one thing," replied the detective sergeant in charge, "a small matchbox in the man's coat pocket, nothing else whatsoever regarding his identity."

"As I expected, he clearly didn't want anyone to know who he was. Would it be possible for me to see the matchbox?" asked Henry.

The DS showed Henry the box which they had placed in a plastic bag to be sent to forensics. He peered at it and was just able to read the name on the cover through the plastic. He was not allowed to touch the box in case there were fingerprints on it.

"It looks like 'Man Man Chi'," said Henry "and there's an address in small letters beneath – it says Wangfujing Da Jie, Beijing."

"I know of that place," replied the DS. "The name means bon appétit or good eating and it's a very popular restaurant. However, there have been reports of illegal deals being carried out there and it is currently under surveillance."

"Sounds as though there's a definite connection between this man and something sinister that might be happening in Beijing."

"Yes, there might well be. I will allow the paramedics to remove the body to the hospital now," said the DS "and arrange for the forensic team to examine the evidence to see if there are any fingerprints that could give us an important lead. Seems like there is a nationwide plot of some kind being hatched."

That's absolutely true, thought Henry as he thanked the DS and made his way back to the winners' enclosure where the presentations were about to be made.

Chapter 24

Shady Dealers in Shanghai

DCI Chan, Sam, Sheba and Cha Li left the Tsim Sha Tsui East ferry pier at noon on Saturday, 15 December, the same day as the Hong Kong Challenge Gold Cup. The seaplane, belonging to the coastguard special forces, was very fast and they soon left Victoria Harbour behind and headed north-east towards the Taiwan Straits, a wide channel of water which separated the large island of Taiwan from the mainland. The plane flew well above the main shipping lane in the centre of the straits and looking down they could see that the mainland coast was dotted with hundreds of small islands around which scores of fishing boats were casting their nets.

Chan began to receive police messages that there had already been several break-ins during the night at the Shanghai Museum and the Jade Buddha Temple – these had already been mentioned in the coded messages. The seaplane flew on over the East China Sea with greater urgency.

It was late afternoon when they arrived in the large estuary which marked the point where the Yangtze and the Huangpu rivers met. A large white lighthouse marked the rocky point where the two rivers met before entering the sea. The seaplane travelled upstream along the Huangpu to the riverfront of Shanghai, China's largest city and seaport with 23 million people. They were met on The Bund – Shanghai's busy seafront and business district, distinguished by its imposing colonial-style buildings. The Shanghai Police escorted them to a well-known landmark, the Peace Hotel, where they had reserved rooms for them to stay and rest after their long journey.

While the girls were escorted to their rooms, DCI Chan wasted no time in catching up with the latest news from Shanghai Police's senior officers. They sat in the internationally famous jazz bar which attracted the world's best jazz musicians and their fans. Inspector Peng informed DCI Chan that some of his officers had been placed in the bar to observe the comings and goings of several suspicious characters who had been meeting there. Chan made a mental note to return there later in the evening. They arranged to meet in the hotel foyer at 7 p.m., once everyone had rested for a couple hours and finished their evening meal.

At 7.30 p.m. Chan and the girls arrived at the Shanghai Museum where they were met by the curator Wu Song. She led them into the galleries which had been roped off to the public, and where the thefts had occurred.

"How many wine vessels have been stolen?" asked Sam.

"Three Shang bronze jias," replied the curator looking very distressed.

"They were very old weren't they?"

"Yes, they dated from the 13th century. But how did you know that the wine vessels had been stolen?"

"They were listed in the coded message that we found."

"Of course," said the curator, "I had forgotten the coded message. It was very clever of you to decode it."

"We all played a part in it," said Sam smiling at the others. "May I introduce my friends, Sheba and Cha Li. It was Cha Li who found the message in the teahouse when we visited the Ten Thousand Buddhas Monastery in Hong Kong."

Madame Wu Song bowed her head and shook hands with Sheba and Cha Li.

"May I ask a question, too?" said Cha Li. "The coded message also mentioned the beautiful Celadon Ware. I looked it up on the Internet and it was breathtaking. It must be so valuable. Has it also been stolen?"

"It is indeed very beautiful and highly valuable and dates from the 12th-century southern Song dynasty. It is heartbreaking to think that… yes, several pieces have been taken. Follow me and I will show you the gallery where they were displayed." Madame Wu Song looked crestfallen.

"Don't give up hope," said DCI Chan. "We will do our utmost to recover them and return them to you."

She smiled wanly, but didn't hold out much hope that the chief inspector's words would come true.

As they walked through the ceramics gallery, Sheba asked how the thieves had managed to break in.

"They somehow disarmed the alarm system during the night and overpowered the night porters. It's never happened before. It must have been very cleverly planned!" exclaimed the curator. "There was one thing I overheard, chief inspector, when the police were talking there earlier. Apparently one of their young officers on patrol last night noticed a suspicious-looking vehicle parked in one of the sidestreets. He may have valuable information for you."

"I shall go and find him right away," said Chan. "May I leave the girls with you for a short while?"

"It will be a pleasure," said the curator with a warm smile.

Chan hastened away and lost no time in finding PC Hanshan

Li. He knew immediately that the young constable was bright and alert.

"I understand you spotted a suspicious-looking vehicle last night," said Chan getting straight to the point.

"Yes, sir, it was a black unmarked van and I noticed that it had a Beijing licence plate."

"Beijing indeed, that's twice that name has been mentioned recently. Did you notice anything else?"

"Yes, sir, it was a rental vehicle and the rental company's details appeared on the windscreen. I made a note of the number and telephoned them first thing this morning. The manager told me that the vehicle had been rented by Mei Jong Antiques dealers who have an antiques shop in the Wangfujing Da Jie shopping district."

"Well, well," said Chan, "this district was mentioned to me by the Hong Kong police this afternoon following an incident at the Sha Tin Racecourse. It looks like we now have two leads. Excellent work PC Hanshan, I shall remember your name when I speak to your senior officers later on."

"Thank you, sir. Oh, and there was one other thing too, sir. I thought it might be a good idea to place a tracker device underneath the vehicle. So now we should know its exact whereabouts."

"I couldn't have done better myself," chuckled Chan as he shook the young officer's hand vigorously.

Later than evening after the girls had gone to bed, DCI Chan returned once again to the jazz bar. He ordered a drink and listened for a short while to the small group of jazz musicians playing one of his favourite pieces, ''S Wonderful' by George Gershwin. There was enthusiastic applause from the audience when they had finished, and Chan then turned to the young barman and asked him if he'd noticed anything unusual in the bar that evening.

"There was one thing," he replied. "Two men dressed completely in black had caught my attention as they sat at a corner table talking in whispers. They wore black raincoats and black leather gloves."

"You seemed to be very observant," said Chan with a faint smile on his lips. "What made you notice the gloves especially?"

"Well," replied the barman, "when they came up to pay the bill, the older of the two men removed his gloves to take his credit card from his wallet. I noticed that there was a small tattoo on the man's right hand."

"Did you happen to notice what it was?"

"Yes, it was in the shape of a cobra."

Chan took a sharp intake of breath before continuing.

"I don't suppose you happened to remember the name of the card holder did you?"

"As a matter of fact I did. You see the man's name was Mei Jong, and the name rang a bell because I have a sister who lives in Beijing and she told me that the other day she visited the Mei Jong Antiques shop in Wangfujing Street near where she lives to purchase an antique Chinese tea set for our mother who celebrated her 50th birthday last week. We agreed to share the cost of the tea set which she saw in the shop window. It was made in 1830 and had a floral pattern printed in blue which we knew our mother would really like, and it was reasonably priced."

Chapter 25

Closing in on the cobramen

DCI Mabon, Huw, Arthur and Ahmed flew from Sheikh Rashid's private airfield near Sha Tin in a north-westerly direction towards the city of Xi'an in Shaanxi province. They had never flown in a private jet before, so it was quite an experience! There were only six passenger seats, plus two for the pilot and co-pilot. They flew at a lower altitude to the larger passenger planes, for safety reasons, and this enabled them to see the landscape below much more clearly. As they approached Xi'an they could see the high peaks of the Hua Shan (Great Flower Mountain) rising to 2,160 metres and the huge loops of the Yellow river as well, which formed the province's eastern boundary.

"Look!" said Huw, pointing down at the two fish-backed mounds at the foot of the mountain range. "Those must be the two mounds mentioned in the third coded message. That's where we must go once we have landed at Xi'an Airport."

"Why do you think they're called fish-back mounds?" asked Ahmed. "Seems a strange description."

"Yes it does," replied Mabon, "and I think it's because the original mound was divided into two parts when they built a new road through it – not knowing at the time it was a sacred burial mound. Fortunately no serious damage was done because most of

Emperor Qin's tomb lies below ground level, so archaeologists have told me."

"That's true," said Arthur, "when Huw and I were shown the model by Emperor Qin and General Tian, we could see the plan was to fill the mound itself with false entrances and passages and make it almost impossible for tomb raiders to find the true entrance."

"And don't forget I suggested they might use spiral patterns when they designed the tunnels to make them as confusing as possible to anyone who got inside," added Huw with a grin and a sideways glance at Arthur.

By this time the private jet was touching down at the outer runway of Xi'an Airport and two police cars were waiting there to take them to the site of the burial mound. As they sped along to the village of Lintong, one of the police officers told Mabon that there had been several attempted break-ins at the mound during the night, but that they had also failed. The tomb raiders had turned their attention instead to one of the excavated pits of the Terracotta Army warriors which had been easier to break into, and they had taken a small number of weapons and other artefacts. The officer said that they had been alerted by a nearby farmer who had been disturbed during the night. Mabon asked if he could speak to the farmer as soon as they reached the site of the mound.

The farmer was waiting for them when they arrived, and took them across his land to the site of the mound where the intruders had attempted to break in. There was nothing much to see, only piles of rubble and red earth where they had been digging.

"They did not get very far," said the farmer with a broad grin on his weather-beaten face. "They must have thought it would be easy, but it's never been done before!"

"So, did they then try to rob one of the pits?" asked Mabon.

"Yes," answered the farmer, pointing to his right where a small huddle of huts stood next to a large excavation. "That is pit number three where the senior officers and commanders of the Terracotta Army were buried."

They followed the farmer to the huts where several archaeologists were busy sorting through a pile of debris. Mabon spoke to Yu Zhong, the senior archaeologist. "Looks as though they've made a horrible mess here too!" he exclaimed after introducing himself.

Yu Zhong stood up and answered Mabon in a distressed tone of voice. "It's heartbreaking for us," he said, "that these thieves can come here and do so much damage to this excavation which we have been working on for several years now."

"I'm so sorry," replied Mabon, "it was thoughtless of me to come barging in like this without fully understanding the extent of the damage."

"It's all right," said Yu Zhong. "You weren't to know how bad it was, and all this for a few bronze weapons, crossbows, swords and daggers, which would not be worth a great amount..."

They could be priceless, Mabon thought to himself.

Chapter 26

Mei Jong Antiques

While Mabon and the boys wandered around the debris at the plundered site looking for clues to the identity of the robbers, DCI Chan decided on a further course of action following his discussions with the young police officer and the barman in Shanghai. He decided to proceed without delay to Beijing, taking the girls with him, and informing the police departments in Hong Kong, Shanghai, Xi'an and Beijing of his plans. They took an internal flight on China Eastern Airlines to Beijing Airport, from where they were transported by police cars to the Regent Hotel in the Dongcheng district. Chan had chosen this hotel because it was only one block away from Wangfujing Street where the restaurant and antiques shop were located. As they had arrived in Beijing during the morning, Chan suggested to the girls that they took a walk to the Suzie Wong restaurant on Wangfujing Street and have lunch there.

"Oh, that would be great," said Cha Li, "and we could do some window shopping on the way." She smiled knowingly at Sam and Sheba.

"I think I've still got some pocket money left that my mother gave me before we left Hong Kong," giggled Sam.

"And I've got some which Sheikh Rashid gave me before he left for the racecourse," laughed Sheba. "So we're all going on a little shopping spree, well that's if you'll let us chief inspector?" She looked up at him with her large appealing brown eyes. How could he possibly say no!

They found a gorgeous department store in the Sun Dong An Plaza, a large shopping mall on the Wangfujing Street which sold just about everything, and it was only a short distance away from the restaurant.

"Right, you've got one hour to browse in the store," said Chan with a broad grin. "Then please join me in the restaurant. Oh, and don't spend too much!" The girls made their way through the store's revolving doors chatting away happily, whilst Chan headed to the restaurant.

The restaurant was a very inviting place, and Chan was welcomed in the foyer by a charming female concierge with long dark hair and wearing a red silk dress embroidered with gold dragons. She explained that there were several themed eating parlours; Chan chose the 'celebrity room' thinking that the girls would like that. The concierge showed him to a table for four and gave him a menu. Chan ordered a drink and explained that his guests would be arriving in a little while. He immediately noticed that the walls were covered in framed photographs of local and international celebrities, many of them stars of film and theatre.

A young waitress approached to see if he was ready to order. "Not just yet," he replied courteously, "I'm waiting for my guests to arrive, in about half an hour or so. There is something I would like to ask you, if I may?"

"Of course, sir, how may I be of help?"

"Would there be a photograph of Mr Mei Jong, the celebrated antiques dealer, somewhere here?" He gestured toward the myriad of pictures on the walls.

"Why yes, sir, there certainly is, would you like me to show you?"

"That would be very kind of you," replied Chan rising to his feet.

She pointed to a section of the wall on the far side. "This section houses photographs of local celebrities and businessmen, and here is a photograph of Mr Mei Jong at a celebratory dinner held here recently when he was presented with a special award for business excellence by the Beijing Business Council."

Chan thanked the waitress and stood for a few minutes looking at the photograph of the elegantly dressed businessman accepting his award with a broad smile, in which there was no hint of the criminal concealed behind it. DCI Chan however knew otherwise. He imprinted the man's face in his memory, the dark slicked-back hair, the black horn-rimmed glasses and the mole beneath the left eye, and then turned to greet the girls who had just arrived carrying their rather large bags of goodies. They were all smiling and giggling happily, and Chan knew that they had enjoyed their shopping spree and he was thankful for that because they had all gone through a difficult time recently, and there was probably worse to come.

"I can see you've all had a good time," he said with a twinkle in his eyes, and the girls all started talking at the same time.

"We've... I've... My..." they all chimed together.

"Hold on now, one at a time, please. Perhaps you would like to go first Cha Li as you seem to have more bags than anyone else!"

Cha Li burst out laughing but then, unexpectedly, handed a bag to Chan. "This is for you," she beamed, "from all of us. You've been so good to us, keeping us safe despite having to cart us half way around China, and through it all you've never once lost your temper with us. You're just like a favourite uncle!"

Chan looked flustered for the first time since he had met the girls. He took out the package and unwrapped it carefully, and then smiled as he looked at a beautifully-framed photograph of the three girls.

"But how..." he blustered, "did you manage to..."

"We asked one of the assistants in the store to take a picture," said Sam, "and we went straight to the photographic department and had it printed and framed."

"Just for you!" said Cha Li and Sheba in unison.

"Thank you all so much," he spluttered, not being used to being spoiled in this way. "I'll always cherish it." He smiled and gestured for them to sit down at the table. There was a lot to talk about, and some of it wasn't going to be related to what the girls had in their own bags. Being a detective meant that he didn't miss much when he was looking around, and he was always discretely observing the other visitors in the restaurant. His eye came to rest on a middle-aged Chinese woman dining alone. She was wearing a uniform of some kind, and he noticed a badge on her short coat. His vision was sharp and he could just about read the words above and below the image of the Ming vase which read Mei Jong Antiques in a stylish oriental script.

"Would you order a meal for us please, Cha Li," said DCI Chan. "There's someone I would like to speak to for a moment."

"Shall I order something for all of us, inspector?"

"Yes please, that would be excellent." He stood up and gave a gentle bow before walking to the woman in uniform. "Excuse me, madam," said Chan, "I could not help noticing your uniform, and I wondered if you could advise me. I am looking for the Mei Jong Antiques shop and in particular I am searching for a very rare piece, a Tang dynasty agate cup. I was wondering if...?"

"That's perfectly all right, sir. I should be very pleased to help you. I shall be here for about an hour for my lunch, and if you so wish I could escort you to the shop when I return there. Where are you sitting please?"

"Just across there!" Chan pointed to the three girls sat at a table where a waitress was already taking Cha Li's order for lunch.

"Thank you, I will give you a signal when I am about to leave. My name is Ho Chong."

Chan bowed his head courteously and returned to his table.

"Well, what delights are we having for lunch then?" he asked.

"Prepare yourself for a real treat," said Cha Li. "Szechuan spring pork and prawn wantons in chili oil, followed by duck spring rolls, and finally orange and green tea loaf cake!"

Chan's eyes were watering as well as his mouth at the prospect of this fabulous lunch. "I hope you have enough money left to pay for it," he said pretending to riffle through his wallet, "I'm just about cleaned out!" He waited for the looks of surprise on the girls' faces.

"But I thought..." stammered Cha Li.

Chan sat in silence, trying to keep a straight face, as the three girls stopped chatting and giggling, and looked at him anxiously.

"Yes, we thought..." said Sam and Sheba.

Chan suddenly burst out laughing. "I was only joking," he said. "I couldn't wait to see the looks on your faces at the prospect of having to pay for the meal when you're already spent out!"

They were all laughing and chatting away merrily when the waitress arrived with the first course. It was a truly memorable meal, and Chan left a generous tip for the waitress when they had finished. He also sent his grateful thanks to the chef.

Outside the restaurant Chan explained to the girls that the

shop assistant he had spoken to in the dining room had offered to take them to the Mei Jong Antiques shop where she worked. A few moments later she walked out of the restaurant and beckoned to Chan and the girls to follow her south along Wangfujing Street. They passed St Joseph's Church on the left, then the Sun Dong An Plaza shopping mall where the girls had spent all their pocket money earlier. Then, just ahead, they could see a large shop sign swaying in the gentle breeze. It was a truly stunning sign which depicted a large blue Ming vase painted in traditional cobalt blue. Above this vase the name of the shop, Mei Jong Antiques, stood out in gold letters which shimmered in the early afternoon light. The sign had been expertly crafted in the form of a hologram so that the lettering and vase painting appeared to change their shapes and could be seen from any angle. It was mysterious and inviting at the same time, indeed just like a cobra waiting to strike.

Ho Chong unlocked the door and invited them into an Aladdin's cave. The girls gasped as they looked around at some of the antiques on display in their high security glass cabinets, and Cha Li led Sam and Sheba towards a well-lit cabinet displaying snuff bottles produced during the Qing dynasty in the 17th century. The bottles seemed to come alive in the bright light and the girls were mesmerized by the delicate figures inside the glass bottles, made from jade, mother-of-pearl, and semi-precious stones such as topaz, onyx and opal.

Chan gestured to the girls that he was going through a beaded curtain into the store room behind the shop which was where a Tang dynasty agate cup was kept under lock and key. He was very privileged to be let behind the curtain, but he had informed Ho Chong that he was a chief inspector after all!

Cha Li wandered over to the reception desk where there was the usual telephone, appointments' book and credit/debit card machine etc., but on the corner of the desk she noticed a rather grubby-looking leaflet. It was a guide to the Forbidden City, and she risked glancing inside wondering what it was doing there. One section was marked off with a squiggly line and some words were underlined and initialled with the letters MJ. She took a sharp intake of breath and mumbled to herself MJ – Mei Jong. But what was MJ's connection with the Forbidden City? She made a spur of the moment decision to slip the guide into her handbook surreptitiously so that she could show it to DCI Chan afterwards. Then she would return it, of course! It could be a clue she thought excitedly.

When they left the antiques shop, Chan was looking a little confused.

"What is it inspector?" asked Cha Li. "You don't look your usual cheerful self."

"Um, no I suppose not," said Chan pulling himself together. He had almost forgotten about the girls for a moment or two, although Sam and Sheba were talking away animatedly about some of the objects of art they had just seen in the shop. "Something wasn't quite right about the agate cup. It should have had a gold stopper in its snout, but it was silver instead, as if it had lost its original stopper. I just felt uneasy about it. You see it's designed in the shape of an ox head." Chan pointed to a picture in the catalogue which Ho Chong had given him, and there it was – a golden stopper forming the nose of the ox's head. It was a beautiful object, and stopped the girls in their tracks as they admired its craftsmanship.

"So does that mean you didn't make them an offer for the cup?" asked Sam.

"Mm, yes that's correct," replied Chan. "I thanked the young lady for her help, but I told her that I would check it out thoroughly before making a decision."

"I'm sure you did the right thing, chief inspector!" Sheba smiled at him and linked her arm in his. "Shall we go back to the hotel now? I think we all need a few hours' rest. It's been an exciting morning, we've had a lovely lunch, but my feet are killing me!"

They all had a good laugh at that, but then Cha Li pulled the grubby leaflet she had picked up from the desk. "You probably need this like a hole in the head, inspector, but before the day is out we may have to visit the Forbidden City."

"What! Have you found a clue?" asked Chan.

"Yes, sir, I think so, and it could be the very thing we've been looking for all along!"

Chapter 27

The Secrets
of the Burial Mound

While DCI Mabon was still busy talking to the senior archaeologist, Huw, Arthur and Ahmed began to walk around the base of Emperor Qin's burial mound. They passed piles of rubble and broken rock where the cobramen had tried to find a way in. They had obviously failed.

Huw looked up towards the summit of the mound, and estimated that it might be around 200 metres high. Recent attempts had been made to camouflage it by planting trees which formed thick clumps in places but, here and there, tracks were visible leading to the top.

"I have a funny feeling that the only way in is up there at the summit," said Huw glancing at Arthur and Ahmed.

"What makes you think that?" asked Arthur, sounding a bit sceptical.

"Well, for one thing, it's the last thing you might think of, and secondly there's a clump of trees at the summit which looks different from all the others, as if they may have been there a long time."

"I think what you are looking at," chipped in Ahmed, "is a stand of bamboo trees. I was reading about China's bamboo forests last night and it seems that they are dwindling fast. If you look carefully you can see that they are taller than the other trees, and their trunks are straight and strong."

"You're on to something there Ahmed," said Huw. "Come on, let's follow this path here, it seems to be leading to the top."

"But what about Mabon?"

"He'll be preoccupied here for a while, and anyway he can always call us on his mobile if he needs us."

"Right let's go!"

Arthur fearlessly led the way along the path, once again in his element as leader of the pack. Huw and Ahmed smiled knowingly at one another, and followed in Arthur's footsteps. They loved it when Arthur was in one of his boisterous moods. Arthur pointed to outcrops of hard rock with crystals that glistened and sparkled in the sunlight.

"Looks like granite," said Huw. "It's very hard and grainy-looking, and some of those crystals are really large."

When they reached the summit they had to work really hard to push their way through the bamboo thicket. Then, right in the middle, they found an open circle with an obelisk in the centre. It was about one-and-a-half metres high, and carved from granite. Chinese letters were engraved onto its six sides, but they were difficult to see as they were overgrown with moss and lichen. Arthur absent-mindedly leant against the obelisk which moved under his weight and a grassed-over trap door opened five metres away on the edge of the circle.

"You've done it again Arth!" shouted Huw. "You're a genius."

They dashed across to the opening and looked down onto a spiral staircase.

"Wow, look at that," said Arthur. "Come on, let's go down there!"

*

Once again he led the way, not in the least bit concerned about what might lie ahead. The others followed gingerly. It was a short spiral staircase, and 25 steps later they were standing on a broad landing. They were at the top of a large dome, and at the end of the landing a marble staircase led down into a large stateroom. It was an incredible sight, and they now understood what the large crystals set in the granite walls of the mound were for. They were the multi-coloured windows. Great shafts of light burst onto the stateroom walls and floor like searchlights, and the effect was breathtaking. As Huw and Ahmed stood on the landing looking down in awe, Arthur was already halfway down the stairs.

"Hold on Arth!" shouted Huw, his voice echoing loudly around the domed stateroom. "You can't just go barging down there like that, this is a sacred tomb, remember."

"Tomb, shshshtoomb," yelled Arthur, as he bounded down the stairs two at a time. In no time at all he stood in the centre of the stateroom.

"Huw... Ahmed!"

"What is it?"

"There's something here you need to see, come on down, this is amazing."

The two boys hurried down to where Arthur was standing in the great stateroom. Huw and Ahmed looked around in wonder at the beautifully-coloured marble from which the entire dome was made.

As they drew closer Arthur pointed down to a large circular glass window in the stateroom floor. Below them was a huge inverted pyramid, with its apex pointing down to the base of the mound. Two staircases led down to the base of the pyramid, one on the west side and one on the east. Huw knew this as he always carried a compass.

Arthur pointed to a door in the wall above the west staircase, and he was off again. The others followed. When they reached the bottom of the west staircase, they were at the upside-down point of the pyramid, and there before them lay the entrance to Emperor Qin's tomb. An archway opened into a chamber lined with gold, and in the centre lay a large plinth on which stood a chariot and four white horses, the resting place of Emperor Qin.

"Don't touch anything," said Huw in hushed tones. "We must find Mabon and the senior archaeologist without delay and tell them what we have found here. It will be for them to decide what is to be done!"

They stood there in awe for a few minutes, gazing in wonder at the sight before them – the emperor's tomb carved from marble, gold and bronze. The details of the construction were astounding in its complexity. The emperor stood erect on the chariot, holding reigns which were tethered to four horses. At his side was a crossbow with a quiver of arrows, and the canopy above his head was shaped like a giant parasol.

"The figure on the chariot even looks like the emperor," said Huw reverentially, with a look of admiration combined with sadness on his face. "We must do all we can to protect this place my friends, but what shall we do next?"

"I know," said Arthur excitedly. "I'll go and fetch Mabon and the archaeologist, and you two can stay here and guard the tomb."

"I'll come back to the summit with you," said Ahmed, "and guard the entrance."

"That's just what I was hoping you'd say," added Huw. "Because I would like to stay here a while and think about Emperor Qin."

Arthur and Ahmed nodded in agreement, and set off back to the entrance at the summit.

Huw sat on a stone ledge at the side of the tomb and contemplated the sight before him. He knew that somewhere beneath the sculpture of the emperor standing on his magnificent chariot lay the mortal remains of the man he had met more than 2,000 years ago when he had travelled back through time. He fingered the jade Buddha which he carried in his pocket and, as he did so, he felt his fingers tingling. The emperor was trying to communicate with him; he knew it instinctively. He took out the figurine and gazed at it, and then he saw the emperor's face smiling back at him.

"Hello, young Huw!" the emperor exclaimed. "I've been listening to your conversation with Arthur and Ahmed, and I am so grateful to you all for trying to protect my resting place against the evil forces of the modern world."

"Oh, your Royal Highness," said Huw. "It's so good to see you again and to hear your voice. Please don't be too fearful about the safety of your tomb, because we will do everything in our power to protect it."

"I know you will, and you have so many good friends and family members to help you. All this I can see from beyond my final resting place. But it will not be easy; indeed it will be exceedingly difficult, and it will test all your resources, courage and strength. So you must be very well prepared and organised when the day of reckoning comes."

"I fear we might be outnumbered," said Huw his confidence weakening when he contemplated the strength and cunning of the cobramen.

"Then you must remember you have my Terracotta Army at your disposal. Hold the jade Buddha tightly and give the command 'Emperor Qin has ordered you to help us!' and then you will not be outnumbered. Oh, and don't forget you must have XCalibur with you when you go into battle with the cobramen. He will have a vital role to play – as you will discover – in more ways than you can possibly imagine. Also you must speak again to Merlin and Draco who will be able to help you in other ways too. Take heart and you will succeed, of that I am sure."

"Thank you, your Highness, I shall remember your advice in the days ahead."

"I must leave you now Huw, as my jade Buddha's energy levels are running low."

Huw noticed that the emperor's image was flickering and was no longer clear and strong.

"Goodbye, sir, and rest in peace. We will not let you down!"

*

Mabon and Yu Zhong were astounded as they descended the spiral staircase into the burial mound. Arthur led the way, with Ahmed bringing up the rear. Mabon looked around in disbelief as they entered the marble stateroom and followed Arthur towards the large circular glass window in the stateroom floor.

"I knew it," said Yu Zhong. "My research had led me to believe that there was a large inverted pyramid inside. I could just about make it out from the infrared photographs we had recently taken. But this is magnificent."

"Come on," urged Arthur. "You ain't seen nothing yet!"

Mabon smiled at Arthur's exuberance, and they followed him with bated breath towards the door leading to the next flight of stairs winding down to the inverted apex of the pyramid. There was an audible gasp from Mabon and Yu Zhong as they entered the emperor's tomb, and gazed upon the chariot and horses on the raised plinth.

Mabon quickly recovered when he saw Huw sitting with his head in his hands. "What is it Huw? Have you been overcome by the sight of all this?"

"No," replied Huw pensively. "It's just that I'm worried now that the secrets of the mound have been revealed. You see I promised Emperor Qin that we would do our utmost to allow him to rest in peace."

"And so it shall be," said Yu Zhong, with respect and authority in his voice. "We have seen all that we need to know, and everything will remain uncovered as it did before. The secrets of the mound will remain hidden – that I promise you!"

Huw brightened up at Yu Zhong's words and after everyone had a good look around the tomb they left carrying only their memories.

Chapter 28

Inside the Forbidden City

DCI Chan and the girls had a much-needed rest in the afternoon following their shopping expedition, lunch at Suzie Wong's restaurant and visit to Mei Jong Antiques. Now they had gathered in Cha Li's bedroom to study the leaflet she had found. It was certainly grubby and well-used, and Chan was certain there would be incriminating fingerprints on it. He had passed it on to forensics immediately on their return to the hotel, and now he was accompanied by Inspector Wan Chei, head of Beijing's forensic department.

"What did you find?" asked Chan, getting straight to the bottom line.

"Well, there are several sets of fingerprints we are very pleased to find," said Na with a broad smile. "You see, we've been on the trail of these thieves for some time, but they are cunning and elusive and very difficult to pin down. We have detained several of them previously, but they always seem to have cast-iron alibis."

"No doubt well planned," said Chan.

"Absolutely, but these fingerprints may lead us to make an arrest if we can also find some of the treasures they have stolen."

"I think this tatty guide to the Forbidden City might be just what you're looking for," chipped in Cha Li excitedly, unable to contain herself. "I noticed also that there were several passages underlined in the guide which might lead you to find what you're looking for."

"Indeed young lady, I wholeheartedly agree with you and well done for spotting this guide in the antiques shop."

"One thing I noticed straight away was that The Hall of Supreme Harmony was earmarked several times and highlighted in yellow too," added Cha Li.

"Sorry to butt in," said Chan with a hint of a smile at Cha Li, "but I remember a case of theft from the Forbidden City which happened several years ago when something was stolen from the screen behind the Emperor Ming's throne. During the search of the throne room we discovered an underground chamber which was never mentioned or revealed by city officials or the trustees of what has become a much-revered shrine and museum. I suggest we begin our search there once we have been granted permission by the trustees."

"I'm sure they'll want to co-operate, chief inspector, as it will be in everyone's interest to expose these thieves," said Na Li.

"There may be much more to it than just theft," said Chan gravely. "The whole of China and the world beyond may be at stake!"

"Are things really that far-reaching?" asked Sam who had been listening intently until now, and as she looked at Sheba she added, "I don't think I fully realised that what we're caught up in is likely to affect everyone worldwide, even though Sheba and I have experienced horrible events before in Dubai and now here."

"I'm sorry if I've alarmed you Sam, but sooner or later you were bound to find out that the cobramen don't operate alone. They are part of a global network of evil men, whatever name you may wish to call them by – thieves, terrorists and extremists. This is the nature of the enemy we are fighting, the cobramen are part of that."

There were sharp intakes of breath all around the room as everyone began to realise fully what they were up against.

DCI Chan's mobile phone rang. It was Mabon, and they could tell from Chan's tone that matters were reaching a head.

"Mabon has asked to convene a meeting of all parties without delay. He and the boys are staying at the Lintong Park Hotel where there is a stable for XCalibur, and we have arranged a meeting for the day after tomorrow, because Sheikh Rashid, Mary, Henry and Mike will need to fly up here too from Hong Kong. I suggest you all have an early night and prepare yourselves for what lies ahead. Events are moving fast, and we must be fully prepared."

*

After dark, and once the girls had gone to their bedrooms, Chan and a few hand-picked officers left the hotel for the Forbidden City. Chan had spoken to the head curator Na Li earlier and he was waiting for them when they arrived. Chan asked the curator to meet them at a little-used side entrance so that they could enter the Palace Museum unobserved and as quietly as possible. The curator led them along a passageway into the largest hall in the palace, The Hall of Supreme Harmony. At the far end sat the ornate throne of the last Ming emperor, dated from around 1420.

Fortunately there were no signs of any members of the cobramen, and Chan moved to the highly-decorated wooden screen behind the throne. He touched the seventh panel of the screen and a trap door opened to the right-hand side, revealing steps down to the basement. Chan led the way into the concealed room, and there by the lights from their torches they could see a large number of treasures which had been stolen from other museums across China.

Na Li was clearly shocked when he whispered, "I had absolutely no idea any of this was here. It's hard to comprehend how anyone could have brought these valuable objects here without us knowing. The museum is well protected and has an excellent alarm system."

"Don't upset yourself," replied Chan quietly. "These men are very cunning and smart, as well as being ruthless. They have no respect for their nation's treasures or its museums, and they will stop at nothing to achieve their evil ends. Their plan would be to sell these valuable objects to the highest bidder, and then to use the money to purchase weapons of mass destruction. Thank you so much Na Li for bringing us here, so that now we have a chance to catch these men and save China's great treasures."

They left the room untouched and made their way back through the throne room to the side entrance where their cars were waiting outside.

Chan was already thinking ahead, and the nucleus of an idea was beginning to form in his mind.

Chapter 29

Setting the Trap

Two days later they were all gathered in the boardroom of the Lintong Park Hotel, which was 21 miles east of the city of Xi'an. It hadn't been easy for DCI Chan to bring everyone together for this important meeting, but now they were all present sitting around the long narrow table with DCI Chan at one end and DCI Mabon at the other. Along Chan's right-hand side sat Cha Li, Sam, Sheba, Huw, Arthur and Ahmed. On his left were Sheikh Rashid, Mary and Henry Grant, Mike Pendry, Na Li, head curator of the Palace Museum of the Forbidden City and, finally, Yu Zhong, the senior archaeologist at Emperor Qin's burial site.

The previous day Chan and Mabon had worked out a provisional plan which was intended to bring the cobramen out of hiding.

Chan began to outline the plan to the others. "Mabon and I have given this a great deal of thought, and we have given priority to ensuring that as little damage as possible is inflicted on Emperor Qin's burial mound which is a World Heritage Site." There were murmurs and nods of approval from around the table.

"Secondly," he continued, "we realised that there are bound to be dangers involved in bringing these evil worms out of the woodwork, but we will ensure that our special police forces will be close by should we need them."

Mabon took up the story. "We have spoken to the chief editor of the *Beijing Herald Tribune* and he has agreed to give full front-page coverage in next Monday's newspaper to the event which we have planned to take place here on the following day, Tuesday. Mr Yu Zhong and the Heritage Trust will announce a new defence system for the burial mound, and work will commence on Tuesday. Temporary fences will be erected, followed by the planting of several rows of trees on embankments to prevent illegal access to the site in future. Chan and I have studied maps of the site in great detail, and we have chosen a large field a mile north of the site, alongside the river Sha for the work to begin. This way we are confident that no damage will be inflicted on the site should a confrontation occur between the tree planters and outside trespassers."

"Thank you most sincerely," remarked Yu Zhong. "We are fearful of any damage to the burial mound, especially following the desecration of the pits housing the Terracotta Army. Your strategy should help considerably."

This time Chan continued. "All temporary road signs will point to the field where the fencing and tree planting will begin. This should lure the cobramen gang to this location, as we firmly believe they will make one last attempt to break into the mound before the new defence measures are in place, and we must be ready for them."

*

The following Monday morning, in a room above the Mei Jong Antiques shop in Beijing a group of men gathered together to listen to their leader.

"I'm sure you will have seen the front page of today's newspaper.

Work will commence to strengthen the defences around Emperor Qin's burial mound near Xi'an, to keep out unwanted visitors like ourselves." Mei Jong was at his sneering best, and the listening group were under his spell.

"I have already alerted the cobramen cell based in Xi'an and preparations are under way for us to make a final assault on the burial mound tomorrow morning. We will leave here by private jet later today to join our comrades in Xi'an, so I would ask you all to be ready to leave by 6 a.m. Do not tell anyone where your destination lies! Is that clear?"

Everyone nodded their heads in agreement.

"I have already sent messages to our comrades in other cobramen cells in adjacent provinces, and they are putting themselves on standby should matters escalate. I have warned everyone to conceal their movements as much as possible until we are ready to strike. We are much more likely to succeed if we can take them by surprise. Let stealth be our watchword – stealth, stealth!" Mei Jong raised his voice as he repeated the watchword.

"Stealth, stealth," hissed the men seated before him.

Mei Jong leered at the group and, knowing that he had them under his power, he enjoyed this moment of glory.

Chapter 30

The Final Battle

It was Monday morning of the following week and the date was 31 December 2012. A team of workers arrived in the large field north of Emperor Qin's ancient burial mound. They quickly set to work erecting fences, digging drainage ditches and setting up diversionary road signs. All visitors and sightseers would have to view the workings from roadside verges. The day passed uneventfully, and the workers made considerable progress.

Tuesday, however, New Year's Day, was a day no-one would ever forget. Unmarked black vans began to arrive on the scene just before daybreak, and dozens of men dressed in black began to cut their way through the perimeter fences which workers had erected the day before. The cobramen had arrived in force, and soon they were moving their weapons onto the field, and making preparations to launch an attack.

DCIs Chan and Mabon had anticipated the cobramen would move in early, and they had positioned themselves on a hill inside the Lintong Park Estate and as dawn broke they surveyed the scene through their powerful binoculars. Although they had anticipated a large force arriving, they were taken aback by the huge numbers assembling and the heavy artillery being moved into place. Chan telephoned headquarters and asked for more reinforcements to be sent, while Mabon called Huw and warned him of the mounting danger. Huw said he would wake up the others and head for the stables without delay.

"What's up?" asked Arthur rubbing the sleep from his eyes.

"Mabon just telephoned to say the cobramen have arrived in the north field."

"What!" yelled Arthur, springing from his bed like a roaring lion. "Why didn't you tell me before?"

"He's only just phoned."

"Get to the stables and prepare the horses!"

"When?"

"Right now."

"Is Ahmed awake?"

"Perhaps you should shake him, and go and tell the girls what's happening too. I'll call the head stable lad and ask him to alert the other lads straightaway. There's no time to lose."

Arthur was already on his way to rouse the others and, in his usual diplomatic way, shouted at them to move their posteriors (or words to that effect)!

It only seemed like minutes before they entered the stables to find the stable lads feeding the horses on fresh watercress, their favourite breakfast food.

"Something strange has happened here during the night," said Ho Song, the head lad.

"What's that?" asked Huw nervously.

"There are six light coats of armour here which have appeared from nowhere, and also special coats of light mail to protect the horses."

"Well, someone up there's looking after us," joked Arthur pointing skywards. "Wherever it came from, let's get it on," he added with his usual broad grin.

Huw smiled to himself and thought about Emperor Qin. He moved quietly towards XCalibur and stroked his neck gently while whispering in his ear. "This is it young feller, this is what we were destined for. Are you ready?" XCalibur nodded his head vigorously, and Huw could see from his large brown eyes that he knew exactly what was going to happen. He stood quite still as Huw placed his usual blanket over his back, followed by the light chain-mail cover and then the saddle. After placing the bridle over his head and fastening the straps in place, he stood back and looked at XCalibur, and suddenly realised what a magnificent horse he was growing into. His white blaze shone against his gleaming black coat, and his eyes were full of fire. As Huw began to don his own light armour, he felt a surge of power within himself that he had not felt before, and he knew that there was a special bond between him and XCalibur which ignited a flame that could not be extinguished. It was eternal.

Once they were fully armed and mounted, they thanked the stable lads, especially Ho Song, who was such an inspiration to the lads and the horses.

"May I lead XCalibur onto the field?" he asked Huw with a big smile on his face.

"Of course you can Ho, it would be an honour for us if you did, and perhaps the other lads would lead the other horses out too!"

Everyone was smiling and chattering away, and for a few minutes it relieved the tension which had been building up. Once on the field the lads retreated back to the stables, leaving the riders and horses to canter to the centre of the south field where the special police forces were already gathering, many of them on horseback. Huw and his five friends looked north towards the place where a large force of cobramen was assembling.

Mei Jong looked south and sneered at the feeble numbers

gathering there. This is going to be a walkover he thought to himself. Soon I will take the treasures from Emperor Qin's tomb and no-one can stop me. Then the power will be mine.

Huw remembered Emperor Qin's advice and took hold of his jade Buddha. He repeated the emperor's decree, "Emperor Qin has ordered you to help us!"

"Where on earth did you come up with that gibberish?" laughed Arthur. "Don't you know the Terracotta Army is made of clay, and anyway they've been buried for a couple of thousand years!"

As Arthur's mocking words ended, there was a huge commotion behind them, and Arthur and the others stood with their mouths wide open as thousands of infantry soldiers and cavalry appeared out of the woods behind the field.

"Not clay any more, Arthur," smiled Huw, as he gazed in awe at the heavily-armoured force gathering behind them. "They've come to life."

"Now we'll see what Mei Jong and the cobramen are really made of," said Ahmed. "I think that evens things up a bit!"

Huw also contacted Merlin using the medallion which he always wore around his neck. Merlin told him to stand firm until he and Draco arrived; they would be there in a matter of minutes and they would appear on a small hillock at the west side of the field to Huw's left. In what seemed like seconds, Huw saw Draco circling the small hill, and Merlin stood there with his long white hair and beard flowing in the breeze. Huw rubbed his medallion hard until Merlin's face appeared in close-up. He was smiling. "There, that didn't take long did it!" he exclaimed.

"I've already seen Draco circling overhead. What do we do now?"

"Wait a few moments and you'll see four more dragons circling above. I have asked the four Chinese water dragons to help us. They live in China's four greatest rivers, the Yellow, Pearl, Yangtze and the Jiang. They are the spirits of the four rivers and they each carry a powerful weapon – water."

"But how can water help us?" asked Huw.

"You will soon see," said Merlin. "I suggest you get ready to lead the charge. Don't give them any more time to organise their weapons. Now is the time to take them by surprise. Oh, and I almost forgot something very important. I want you to rub XCalibur's blaze with your left hand and take up your sword in your right hand."

"Right, I'm doing that now, and oh, something strange is happening – XCalibur is nodding his head vigorously and I can feel a strong flow of energy surging through my body and up my right arm into my sword."

"That's good!" exclaimed Merlin. "Now brace yourself for what comes next."

Huw gripped his horse tightly with his legs and looked up as he saw Draco flying towards him. A long flame leapt from the dragon's mouth and enveloped Huw's sword which was held aloft. He could feel the intense heat from the flame, but only the sword was engulfed. As Draco flew past the flame evaporated and the burnished sword gleamed in Huw's hand. He gasped as he realised that he was no longer holding an ordinary sword. It had been metamorphosed in the heat of the dragon's flame into King Arthur's EXCALIBUR.

Huw, Arthur, Ahmed, Cha Li, Sam and Sheba looked up in astonishment at the mighty sword held high in Huw's grasp. It was dazzling as it reflected the rays of the morning sun, and it seemed to encompass them all in a ball of light. It was a force field, and Huw knew instinctively what he must now do. He led his courageous friends to the front of the assembled army. Their fears were gone, and they felt brave and strong inside. The spirit of the dragon lived inside each one of them, and they felt invincible.

"I've never felt like this before," said Sheba, who was usually the quietest and most reserved of the three girls.

"Me, neither," added Sam, "although I've been in some tight corners before."

"I feel great," exclaimed Cha Li with a flourish of her sword, "bring it on!" She was her usual exuberant self again.

"Forward," shouted Huw, pointing Excalibur straight ahead towards the enemy. They began at a trot and quickly increased their speed to a canter.

Chan and Mabon trained their binoculars on Mei Jong and his officers. They looked completely startled by the sight of the cavalry already advancing toward them.

"This is not right," shouted Mei Jong in a frustrated tone. "We were supposed to take them by surprise." He knew they had been outwitted, but he gritted his teeth and barked an order. "All guns in the front line – fire at will." The order quickly passed down the line and soon the shells were whistling overhead.

"Charge!" yelled Huw and the horses were now at full gallop. Behind them thundered the horses of the Terracotta chariots and the Special Police cavalry. Ahmed blew loud sounds on his Arabian horn which seemed to rouse everyone, and soon the air was filled with battle cries.

Shells began to explode around them, but they seemed to ricochet off the force field that surrounded Huw and his friends, and the explosions did no damage. Mei Jong was mystified to see that the explosions were having little effect, so now he moved his tanks to the front line. They had even more powerful guns.

Huw pointed his sword upwards toward the water dragons circling overhead, and then something totally unexpected happened. The dragons swooped down over the north field, and released torrents of water from their open mouths. A huge wall of water, like a tsunami, swept across the tanks and guns of the cobramen. The tanks filled with water and none of the guns were able to fire. Large numbers of invaders were drowned and swept away into the river Sha.

Mei Jong rallied his men on high ground to the right flank, then ordered them to attack with assault rifles and hand guns. Huw gave the signal for the Terracotta infantrymen to come through to the front line, and there they assembled in squares with their shields for protection. Bullets from the assault rifles came thick and fast, but most bounced off the thick bronze shields. Soon the cobramen had run out of ammunition and had to resort to hand-to-hand combat using iron bars and fence posts. They were no match for the trained infantrymen of the Terracotta Army and their broadswords.

Mei Jong stood on high ground to the rear of the combat zone shouting orders to his men, but keeping well out of the trouble himself.

Huw felt his medallion vibrate, and looked at it to see Merlin's image again. "Hold Excalibur in your hand as if it was a spear, and then throw it with all your might at Mei Jong!"

Huw followed Merlin's advice and the sword leapt from his hand and sped forward with the speed of lightning. It became white hot and emitted a high-pitched whine as it zoomed in on its target like a homing missile. As it passed over the men in combat, they dropped their weapons and covered their ears to shut out the piercing shriek of the sword in flight.

Mei Jong was rooted to the spot as Excalibur struck, spearing him through the chest right up to the hilt. He fell back with a look of horror on his face, and the last thing he saw was the face of the dragon etched on the hilt of the sword.

The battle was over and as the soldiers of the Terracotta Army waved their swords and cheered, the Special Police Force rounded up the remainder of the cobramen and led them to the waiting police vans to be taken into custody.

*

Merlin took charge of the victors in the centre of the battlefield. He asked them to assemble in a large circle and then, with Huw's permission and help, climbed up onto XCalibur's back.

"This is a very special young horse," he said patting XCalibur's neck, "and these young people who showed great courage leading you into battle today – they are very special too!"

There was a loud cheer from the assembled crowd. Merlin raised his hand to quiet them. Then he asked Huw, Arthur, Sam, Ahmed, Sheba and Cha Li to hold hands and form an inner circle.

"This struggle has been going on for a long time now, and I fear it is not over yet, but I raise my sword in salute to this 'circle of six' young men and women who are our futures. May this circle continue to grow in number until it reaches all the way around the world so that children and young people from all nations and faiths will join together to defeat the forces of evil and bring peace to planet Earth."

End Notes

Deciphering
the Coded Messages

First Coded Message:
This is a mirror image of the message, so hold it up to a mirror to read its secrets.

Second Coded Message:
Each letter in the message is the one that precedes the actual letter in the alphabet, so R is replaced by Q, E is replaced by D, and so on.

Third coded Message:
This is probably the world's most famous code: The Morse Code, devised by American inventor Samuel Morse. Each letter has a symbol(s) e.g. A= .- B= -..., and can therefore be written down symbolically *or* messages can be sent long distance using electrical impulses to represent dots and dashes.

If you are interested in reading more about codes and messages see *Codes and Ciphers*, a Collins 'gem' book published by Harper Collins Ltd.

Also available, the first two books of the trilogy:

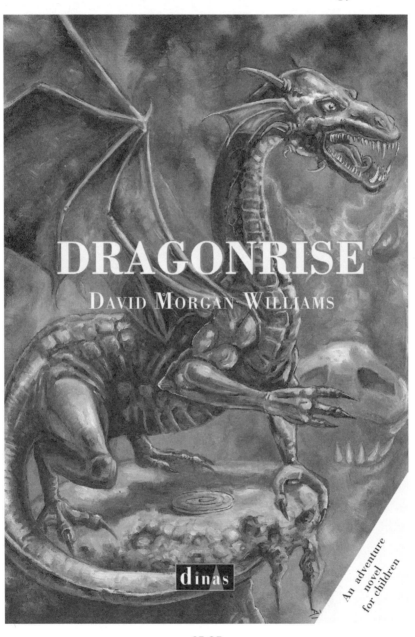

DRAGONRISE

DAVID MORGAN WILLIAMS

dinas

An adventure novel for children

£5.95

Ebony
and Ivory

David Morgan Williams

y Lolfa

£5.95